The Love of Good Women

:002

2

02

Also by Isabel Miller from The Women's Press:

Patience and Sarah (1979)
A Dooryard Full of Flowers (1994)
Side by Side (1996)

ISABEL MILLER

The *Love* of Good Women

Published in Great Britain by The Women's Press Ltd, 1995
A member of the Namara Group
34 Great Sutton Street, London EC1V 0DX

First published in the United States of America by The Naiad Press,
Inc, 1986

First published in Great Britain by Black Swan, 1989

The quote on page 114 is from 'My Heart Leaps Up When I Behold'
by William Wordsworth.

The hymn on page 184 is from 'O Sometimes Gleams Upon Our
Sight' by John Greenleaf Whittier, 1852. It is sung here to the tune
'Hamburg'.

An early version of the first Gray Oaks flashback was published as a
story by *Aphra* magazine.

British Library Cataloguing-in-Publication Data
A catalogue record for this book is available from the British Library

ISBN 0 7043 4447 5

Printed and bound in Great Britain by BPC Paperbacks Ltd,
Aylesbury, Bucks

To all the women
of all my consciousness-raising groups,
who taught me many things--
some of which I did not
want to know

FOREWORD: MILLY

In those days, Milly was in danger of loving any woman who held out her hand and some who didn't. Earl's wife Trude, for instance, didn't, but Milly went into a spin anyway, scared as always because these things always hurt and nothing ever came of them, not even a kiss. The world conspired to guarantee that. But Milly had learned to get the good of love, the wonderful leap and sweetness in the chest during the little while when it wasn't committably insane to hope. Life would go back to hard and gray again, but she was used to that. She had, she liked to think, broad shoulders.

Anyway, it was too late. One look at Trude, and Milly began to fantasize throwing a blanket over her head and kidnapping her. That way it wouldn't be Trude's fault and she wouldn't have to feel guilty. A cabin in the northwoods. Re-education. Trude, say one hundred times every day, "I have a right." Bringing that one small, timid, virtuous, ignorant, brown-haired, awkward country woman to the knowledge of her own beauty, to love and power, would be Milly's life work. That's one for my side, world. You've drowned our baby girls, you've sealed our maidens into towers and chastity belts, you've beaten and raped and killed and despised and trivialized us, you've set us against each other, but by God here's one you don't get. Here's, in fact, two.

Then reality had to stick its big nose in. In reality, Milly was shy and Trude was mysteriously attached to Earl. Trude seemed impossible. Sometimes Milly thought the kindest thing would be to put her painlessly out of her pain.

In her despair, Milly forgot: Just as the longest drought will end in rain and the longest war will end in peace, the longest worm can turn and, with a little help from its friends, stand up and bite.

BOOK ONE: GERTRUDE

While there was still snow in the north shadow of the house, the crocuses blossomed, and Gertrude thought, Oh, why didn't I do it in crocuses? Tulips take so long. But the crocuses withered in a flash, and there were the tulips just coming up, chewy fat green leaves with smudges of red, all the best part of their lives still ahead of them, and Gertrude knew she'd chosen right.

She watched the tulips every day and didn't tell anyone. She told the children, because heavens she couldn't keep absolutely quiet about such a thing, but she didn't tell Earl. Every bulb was good. Every cluster of leaves had its hard green little bud folded and waiting, and soon the stems shot up long and the buds softened, and on the day they split and let her see the color inside she decided not to wait any more. Why should she? Why should she keep such a thing to herself, now that the pattern was clear and anyone could see it?

She would have a little family party—a garden party—and let Earl's first look at the tulips be the high point. She could hardly wait to see his face. All day while she raked, and scrubbed the porch, and brought the lawn furniture out of the barn and scrubbed it too, she saw Earl's face. Picturing his face shining with unbelief and joy gave Gertrude the strength to use the last grain of the sugar ration for cookies and lemonade. War or no war, this was no day to be stingy.

The girls would look like blond angels in their white organdy dresses. Earl Junior would be neat and clean. Gertrude herself would look—adequate. And Earl—Earl always looked wonderful, so tall and distinguished and tailored. They would all sit on the porch together, a happy family, sipping lemonade with murmurs of appreciation, praising the cookies, and then Gertrude would say, "Let's walk around and see what's coming up," and there'd be the tulips, and Earl's face.

When the children came home from school, Gertrude made them wash and put on their good clothes. She did what she could about their shoes. She polished them, but they were still brown school shoes, walked-over at the heels. She felt the unfittingness of wearing such shoes with white dresses. Her children were, after all, Earl's: aristocrats. And maybe Gertrude didn't have their natural inborn good taste but she did have some, and she did know you need white shoes with white dresses. The shortest look at any catalog would teach anybody that much.

Oh, if only, if only. Just a little more, God? Not for herself but for the children, so they could take the place in life they were born to? Not wealth—she wasn't greedy—just enough for white shoes for the girls?

Poor Earl was making all the money a decent, honest man could. The way to make money was not to care whose toes you step on, and Earl just wasn't made that way. She was glad he wasn't, but since he wasn't, where would the white shoes come from? Would fairy shoemakers come in the night? Tap tap all night with their tiny hammers? Gertrude could almost hear them. Would ravens come, dangling white shoes by white shoestrings from their beaks? She wouldn't have admitted it, but she didn't entirely set aside the possibility.

One thing she knew, she wouldn't get a job. Her job was at home, making her family happy. If only she could earn while staying home. Could she take in sewing? Really, you had to live in town for that. Could she sell tatted handkerchiefs? Maybe.

Well, something would come. There was a great demand for tatting. Nurses liked tatted handkerchiefs in their pockets to add a touch of color. And *every*body liked tatted doilies, especially the frilled ones that stood up around a vase or ornament like the fancy collar around Sir Walter Raleigh's face on the tobacco can, only better yet than that, being all-colored and lacy. Tatting for sale was very likely the answer. Earl's daughters would have white shoes.

She brushed their hair and looked at Earl Junior. Poor little monkey, he did look out of place with his dressed-up sisters. He should have a little white suit, and, yes—white shoes too. Surely God could see that, when even Gertrude could.

She scrubbed the shoe polish off her hands with scouring powder. She didn't wish for automatic hot water, but she did wish the faucet labeled HOT would go away and stop reminding her. Then she went to dress.

Poor scrawny body, but what could you expect at age thirty-six? And some women's tummies stuck out and lopped over like old old bosoms, and certainly that was worse. The catalog had pictures to prove it, and wide canvas belts with bones and laces for sale to fix it. Gertrude showed them to Earl sometimes, to make him glad she was scrawny, but showing him usually backfired because then he'd go on and look at the rest of the ladies' undergarments and make little cries and moans and smack his lips quite loud and look at Gertrude with regret. But in the end he'd be sweet and say he was *glad* she was built like an ironing board, because it saved a lot of money that might otherwise be spent on brassieres and corsets, and a man can get used to anything. That was his teasing way, and Gertrude liked it better than a lot of sentimental mush that would only have embarrassed her, she guessed.

She was snapping the placket of her blue organdy dress when she heard the eek of brakes that meant Earl was home. She felt hurried and frazzled. There was no time to do her bun over. Well, her mother had always told her that she looked better before she combed her hair than after. Before, there was still hope. Gertrude glanced quickly and sadly at the mirror. It was too small and too high, set right for Earl. She didn't care. She didn't want to know.

She hurried outside. The children were dragging Earl toward the tulips, saying, "Daddy, Daddy, come see!" Oh, they made her cross. He wasn't supposed to see the tulips *yet*. Well, rather than let them be the ones to show him, as though *they'd* turned a hand to help her! she'd have to change the plan a little. Maybe it wouldn't matter.

"Come see, come see!" she said.

"God, what a day!" he said.

"Oh, this'd make *any* day seem nice. Come see."

He groaned and followed.

"Shut your eyes, now," she said. "I'll lead you."

"Can I trust you?"

But he shut his eyes and she led him. She tried standing him different places, first here, then there. His first look had to take in the whole. When she had him in just the right place, she said, "There! Open!"

"So I open," he said.

The children almost spoiled everything. They couldn't wait until he saw for himself. "It spells our name, Daddy! It spells Sunup, look, Daddy, look, here's the S."

Gertrude could tell from Earl's expression that he could not believe his eyes.

"Your taste, peasant lass, is—tantamount, as always."

She didn't know what that big word meant, but she knew it must be something good. It was nothing against her that she didn't know as many words as Earl. Why, *no*body knew as many words as Earl. She had seen very very intelligent and educated people, such as Earl Junior's teacher, just sort of sit there blinking when Earl came out with one of his words.

Gertrude smiled. "The S is in 'General French,'" she said. "That's red, you see the streaks of color there? The U's in 'Ellen Wilmot,' that's yellow. The N's—"

"Yes, yes. Tell me the rest later. I can't take in so *much*. Break it to me gently."

She laughed. She loved having him so jolly and jokey. The children were dancing around the edge of the tulip bed. "Be careful, don't step on the flowers," she called.

"Don't step—*jump*," Earl said.

She began to wonder.

"If you don't like it, I can dig them up," she said, to show that she could joke too.

"It won't be necessary. I can easily run over them with the lawnmower."

Was he teasing or not? It was so hard to tell. But he probably was. He just about had to be. When did he ever have time to mow the lawn?

He said, "I'm kidding, of course."

"You do like it, don't you?" she asked.

"Well, all in all, no, now that you pin me down."

Oh.

They walked up the lawn toward the porch. If only the children hadn't spoiled the plan. If only they'd waited and let Earl relax and have his lemonade, then he'd have liked the tulips. Who could enjoy anything, come at like that after a hard day's work?

She said, "I planned it out way last fall. You have to plant tulips the fall before, you know. I'm sorry. I thought you'd like it."

"I wonder what made you think that."

"You said—last fall—remember that day we went for the ride—we saw a place with a name like that in flowers. I thought you liked it."

"I doubt it. I don't remember, but I doubt it."

"Oh, you said so. I remember. You said, 'One thing we know about whoever did that, he's *persistent*.' "

"You think that over, Gertrude."

"Oh, I don't know. What *do* you like? I try. I never know."

"It's very simple, Gertrude. I like money. And, let's see—money, and—uh, money, and did I mention *money?* and last but by no means least, money. When you're asking yourself will Earl like this? will Earl like that? will Earl like Sunup spelled out in tulips? just ask yourself, is there money in it? How much money will Sunup spelled out in tulips put in Earl's pocket? Would Earl *Henderson* Sunup spelled out in tulips put any *more* money in Earl's pocket? I hope I haven't confused you. Is it molar enough? I like money. I don't know any easier words to say it in, I'm sorry to say."

Gertrude couldn't be hurt when he put it all so cute, and she knew he didn't mean it. He was poking fun at himself, being modest, refusing to say he had a worthwhile reason for anything he did. As a loving father, he wouldn't blame the children. And out of consideration for her feelings, he kept back his other reason, which, thinking it over, she could easily see was his aristocratic taste. How ugly the tulips must have seemed to an aristocratic taste like Earl's. Red next to yellow! How tactful he was, how careful of her feelings, pretending he was money-mad when his whole life proved he wasn't at all.

He sat down on the porch in the big woven chair with the high heart-shaped back. The girls in their pretty dresses gathered around him. They were a sight to gladden any heart except that their bright hair showed how merely brown his was now. Well, he would always be Golden Earl to Gertrude, no matter what.

Gertrude brought glasses enough for all. "Girls, help your mother," Earl said. She was glad he said it, but she didn't need help. Next she brought the frosty pitcher clanking with ice, and then (another trip) the plate of cookies, and then at last Earl's slippers.

"Mama, this lemonade's too sour."

"There's not enough sugar in the cookies, Mama."

"Gertrude, a touch of gin would save the lemonade. Will you bring out the bottle, please?"

She brought the gin, and sat down in the wooden rocker beside Earl.

"We all look nice except Mama, don't we?" Ruby said. (Ruby was the tactless one.)

Earl said, "Ruby, that will do. Your mother is entitled to common courtesy."

Gertrude said, in haste, to prevent her tears of gratitude from falling and embarrassing him, "What kind of a day did you have, Earl?"

"I've already told you twice. I am drained. I am absolutely drained."

"Here, take my chair to put your feet up on. I'll sit here on the step."

"Red-necked Georgia crackers all day long, their ham

hands bulging with ready cash, their noses going twang twang twang. 'Waall, Mistuh Sunup, suh, ah'll make it wuth yore whahl, you git me a cah and ah'll make it wuth yore whahl.' They could, too. And I haven't a single car on the lot. God, it drains me. Gertrude, would you like to know where those crackers are getting that ready cash? They're working at Spragg Enterprises. That is, they're scratching their private parts and punching a time clock, for three dollars an hour. Spragg's has made this town the Mecca of every cracker in the South. As I said to August Spragg at luncheon today, 'August,' I said, 'thanks to you, when I walk down the streets of our once-fair city, I almost think I'm back in Gray Oaks, Florida.' "

"Really, Daddy? Really, Daddy, did you say that to August *Spragg*?"

"After all, I went to college with August."

"You did? Oh, boy!" Earl Junior yelled. He jumped up, full of the terrible pep that made everybody so nervous. (He was the peppy one.) He couldn't stay still. He had to run around, jump around, walk the porch rail, fall off, land laughing, jump up laughing, yelling, "Us Sunups must be pretty smart!"

Gertrude was surprised. She thought he knew about all that already. Earl seemed to be feeling mixed emotions. How could he help but be pleased, in a way, and yet, of course, like any good father, anxious to nip Earl Junior's cocky conceit in the bud? Earl dutifully said the things that would bring Earl Junior back to earth, even though it meant bringing himself down at the same time.

"Well, that was a long time ago," Earl said. "There he is and here I am."

"But we *are* smart, aren't we? Aren't we? You're as smart as August Spragg. You went to *college* with him."

"There are differences. He married money. I married

your mother. His father made money. My father lost money. Need I go on?"

"We *are* smart. Look at Uncle Barney!"

"*You* look at Uncle Barney."

Gertrude said, "Barney's been a godsend for us, Earl."

"I've been a godsend for Barney, damn it. I'm the one that keeps Barney going. Did anybody ask if I'd like to volunteer too? No, it has to be Barney that gets to play sailor boy and play hero, because good old Earl will keep the garage running. To hell with Barney. For two cents I'd run a lathe for August Spragg."

Gertrude wanted to wring Earl Junior's neck. What was the matter with that boy anyway? Well, whatever was the matter, she couldn't straighten him out, not now, not with dinner to get. She hoped he was satisfied. He'd spoiled the garden party mood, upset Earl, got himself dirty falling off the porch rail. She gave up. She just washed her hands of that boy.

"I have to go cook now," she said. "And it wouldn't hurt you great big girls to help me. You too, Earl Junior."

"Help your mother," Earl said. They all trooped to the kitchen, leaving Earl alone on the porch. There wasn't anything for the children to do because Gertrude had everything almost ready ahead of time. She had to do everything alone. The children were no help at all.

"Go sit on the back porch and try to behave," she said. "Don't get dirty."

They went out and perched in a row on the back steps. They were no help at all. They could have at least set the table. Ione could have stayed with Earl, but no.

"Ione!" Gertrude called. Ione came in. She was sixteen, and taller than Gertrude. "See if you can cheer Daddy up a little," Gertrude said.

"I'll see if he wants to play croquet," Ione said.

"Oh, no, don't ask him that," Gertrude said. (Ione was the charmer, but there were limits.) "Just—jolly him up somehow. You know how."

Ione did know how. How she did it, Gertrude would never understand. Ione could twist Earl around her little finger. She was the one Gertrude depended on when something had to be got out of Earl. Ione even got him to take the family for that ride last fall. She was born knowing more about men than Gertrude had learned in all these years of trying, or ever could learn. Yet it wasn't all cleverness on Ione's part, exactly. There was just something about her that Earl liked, which was lucky for Ione because at least one parent ought to like her and Gertrude, unfortunately, the secret shameful truth to tell, didn't much—couldn't—try as she might. There was just something *about* Ione.

Maybe it was the same something that Earl liked. Whatever it was, Ione hadn't been on the porch with Earl for two minutes before Gertrude heard him laughing. It was kind of too bad, it was almost unfair, that Earl couldn't enjoy his other children that way. If only Earl could feel some of the pleasure Gertrude felt in the others. Earl was missing so much, not enjoying fine manly peppy little Earl Junior, and Ruby and Tamar so helpful and thoughtful and obedient. It was Gertrude's fault, for not giving them a chance to shine. She would do it at dinner.

"I wonder what other people are having for dinner," Gertrude said, to open an interesting topic.

"I wonder what we're having," Earl said, looking at the escalloped potatoes in his serving spoon, pretending to be confused. Such a good joke; the children screamed with laughter, and even Gertrude smiled.

"What is it, what is it?" the children asked. How they giggled.

"I think it's—rattlesnakes!" Earl Junior said.

Earl laughed.

"Oooh, icky!" the girls squealed.

Earl laughed.

"I think it's rattlesnakes," Earl Junior said.

"A little too gray for that," Earl said.

"It is, it's rattlesnakes!"

"It couldn't be. They're out of season," Earl said.

"*Rattlesnakes!*"

Laughter. All so jolly and pleasant. If only all their meals could be like this.

"Rattlesnakes coin-sliced like carrots," Earl said. "Served in dirty cheese sauce." He was steadily dishing-up during all this. The plates went around the table hand to hand.

"Don't give *me* no rattlesnakes!" Earl Junior said.

Earl said, "I've had enough out of you! Just for that, you leave the table."

Earl Junior sobered down immediately but didn't move.

"You heard me," Earl yelled. "Do you want this spoon in your face? Don't tempt me, boy!"

Earl Junior began to cry and left the table. Such an impossible boy. He always managed to keep at people until they lost their tempers.

When dinner was over, Ione said, "Let's play croquet, Daddy."

Gertrude held her breath and looked down at her plate, bracing herself for Earl's no, not wanting to see the girls' faces when he lashed out. Why couldn't they learn to read the signs before they rushed in? "Croquet! Croquet!" the girls yelled. What a noise.

Gertrude braced herself, but Earl said, "Might as well. Might be fun." And off they all went to the back yard. All the while she was washing dishes, Gertrude could hear the wonderful heart-warming noises of their happiness—the tunk of the balls, the girls' squeals, Earl's laughter. When the dishes were done, Gertrude sat on the back steps with her apron wrapped around her arms and watched. Who'd think they were poor? Who'd ever guess, seeing this elegant scene? And it was Gertrude who made those dresses as nice as store-boughten, Gertrude who skimped herself to let Earl go tailored, Gertrude who had planted that bright green grass. These were the moments that made everything worthwhile.

Then Earl Junior whispered from inside the door, "Mama." It was wrong to undermine Earl's discipline, but she went inside without making a fuss. "Mama, I'm hungry," he whispered. She felt sorry for him even though he had spoiled her day. He didn't look much like a Sunup right then, or even peppy. He just looked miserable and tacky, with his face puffy from crying.

She gave him the leftover potatoes—there were quite a few—and he took them gratefully. He looked so forlorn she almost felt like putting her arm around him, but they weren't a mushy family so she didn't. He wouldn't have liked it.

"They're having a lot of fun out there, aren't they?" he said.

"You be a good boy and next time you can have fun, too," she said. It was the least she could say to support Earl, after going behind his back this way.

Watching Earl Junior gulp down the cold potatoes almost made her sad, so she went outside to watch the croquet.

It was hard to remember sometimes that all these graceful aristocratic children had once been her very own little babies, looking to her for everything, burping against her shoulder, leaning their fuzzy wobbly heads against her throat. It was only right that they should turn to Earl as they grew older, but sometimes she wished, in spite of everything, that she could have a baby again, to love.

She might have started feeling sorry for herself at that rate, but luckily it was time for Lux Radio Theater. She was listening to it when darkness drove her family into the house. Earl was so nice. He didn't change the station or anything. He sat down and listened. They all sat there in such a happy little circle around the radio, for the first time since Gertrude couldn't remember when. The story was so wonderful, about a sissy boy who became a man in the Army. That sissy boy even got so he didn't have to wear glasses any more because he wasn't spoiling his eyes reading. Then Cecil B. DeMille came on and said, "Goodnight—from—HOL-ly-wood," and then a different announcer said, "Patriotic Americans! Men! Women! Uncle Sam needs *you* in war plants and industries, to stand shoulder to shoulder with our gallant fighting men! Help give our brave men the planes, the guns, the ships they need! 'Give us the tools, we'll do the job!' they say. 'We can ax the Axis. We can slap the Japs.' Can *you* refuse them?"

Earl gave Gertrude a look. She felt sure there was a meaning in that look.

Did he think that message, that plea, was for her? Why, it couldn't be. It was for the fat lazy goodfornothing women who spent their whole days painting their fingernails and playing bridge, neglecting their few little spoiled-rotten children, opening some cans a few minutes before mealtime, never putting wholesome food on the table. Gertrude was speechless. What could Earl's look mean? Did he want her to get a job?

"Bed now, brats," Earl said. The girls crowded around him and kissed him and went off to bed like lambs. Gertrude was so glad when he took hold and disciplined the children. They never obeyed her that way. She had to hit them, sometimes, to make them go to bed, but Earl never even had to raise his voice.

"What did you mean by that look you gave me?" she asked. He held his finger to his lips and gestured toward the radio. She'd have to wait until the new program was over to ask him. To fill the time, she gathered up the girls' dresses and set them to bleach. She took as long as she could about it, but he was still listening to the radio when she got back to the living room.

"That about how you like money, was that—"

He held his finger to his lips and stopped her. He made a silent drinking gesture. She brought him the gin bottle.

"Did you mean Spragg's—"

He wouldn't let her talk. He sat there drinking, shushing her, listening to just anything on the radio—static, ads, rebroadcasts. He was just crazy about the radio.

She got out her ironing board and ironed her large tablecloth. She wanted to sew, but the noise of the machine bothered Earl so she didn't dare. She worked away at her tablecloth. It didn't come out right. The edges didn't line up together when she folded it. She sprinkled it and ironed it again. "Earl—"

"Shhh."

She'd just have to wait until every last station went off the air. She washed the girls' dresses and ironed them while they were still wet. That took a long time. While she was finishing up the last dress, "The Star-Spangled Banner" came on.

"Earl—"

"Shhh." He listened until the last note died away, and then he listened to the silence for a while, and then he turned the knob everywhere, everywhere, and listened to other stations playing "The Star-Spangled Banner" and then he listened to a preacher for a while but the preacher at last was too much and Earl snapped off the radio and stood up and went off to bed, so tired that he accidentally kicked over the empty gin bottle.

A chance to talk, at last.

"Do you think I ought to get a job? Now that the children are all in school? I could work nights maybe?"

Yawn. "Up to you."

"But do you think I should?"

"Up to you."

If only she knew what he wanted. Whenever she knew what he wanted, she did it in a flash.

She said, "Seems to me my main job's right here, taking care of the family. Cooking."

"Sliced rattlesnakes," he said, smiling pleasantly, his eyes closed.

"Do you mean I might as well not cook?"

Yawn. "I don't mean anything."

"Just tell me, Earl. I'll do it if you want me to. I just don't want to do it and have you say I shouldn't of."

No answer. The fact was, he didn't like to take the blame if things went wrong, either. He was dozing. Was he pretending? No, he was grinding his teeth, which he couldn't do while awake. He could snore awake or asleep, but he couldn't grind his teeth unless asleep.

Well, whether he said plain-out or not, she knew, because she was a real wife and knew his wishes, sometimes even before he knew them himself. It was mysterious, how she knew. It wasn't Earl's way to be bossy, bless his heart. He'd told her as plain as his way allowed. She would get a job at Spragg Enterprises, and forget about tatting. Nobody appreciated handwork any more, anyway.

Having her mind made up relaxed her. She curled up in the little part of the bed Earl wasn't sprawled on. There was no use trying to get him to move when he'd been drinking, but she didn't feel cross. She felt grateful that if he had to drink he did it at home this time and spared her the worry. How she worried when he was out. She could never rest those times, for thinking of all that might be happening to him. She couldn't stand it if even one hair of his head was in danger, and it was agony to think that he might be wandering into the river and drowning, or he might be bleeding somewhere from a car accident, terribly cut. But no such fear tonight. She could be comfortable in the tiny space he left her, as long as she knew he was safe, that the phone wouldn't ring, the policeman wouldn't say, "Mrs. Sunup? I'm afraid we've got kind of bad news for you."

* * * * *

Earl waited for Gertrude the next morning while she did the few little necessary things—washed the breakfast dishes, made the beds—and that was proof again that he wanted her to work at Spragg's. True, he did *pretend* he wouldn't wait, and sat in the car racing the motor, but he did wait and that was proof all right.

He was cross. He didn't thread the car between the holes in the road but rammed his way straight through, and pretty fast, complaining, "You made me late, you made me late."

She knew better than to say anything. She just kept quiet and looked out the window, feeling sorry, and half sick with nervousness about Spragg's, and feeling also, she couldn't understand why, excited and happy. Something about the bright spring sunshine, something about the little glimpses into other people's lives—the woman shaking a rug from an upstairs porch, the little collection of lunch buckets beside the schoolbus stop and the boys the buckets belonged to playing catch—*some*thing made her feel, oh, the *real*ness of life. And riding through the edge of town, she saw even more life being real. She felt her heart getting bigger and fuller to take everything in—there was a mailman, there was a milk wagon pulled by a horse, there was a storekeeper cranking his awning down—and then Earl said, "Here's Spragg's," and her heart gave one snap and withered back to normal.

Oh, Spragg's was large. It was low, one-story, red brick with blue windows, surrounded by a fence so long that it disappeared over the horizon like railroad tracks. Enormous. It was the largest building in the world. She pleased Earl by saying so, and he said, "Oh, that's nothing compared to Willow Run, now *there's* a *large* plant." Larger than Spragg's? Well, if Earl said so.

"Here's the main gate," Earl said. "Ask one of the guards where to go."

"Oh, Earl—"

"It's up to you."

"Oh—"

But she got out and Earl immediately drove away so there was no turning back. She told the guard she had come for a job, and that was the only hard part. After that, all she had to do was follow along, follow directions. There were about twenty other people, men and women, after jobs that same day. She supposed they'd all heard Lux Radio Theater and that plea and were here for patriotic reasons, just like her.

They were fingerprinted and photographed and given the oath of allegiance. A doctor listened to their hearts. Another doctor lined them up and said if they'd ever had any mental problems to raise their hands, and then he went along the line and glared at each person. Gertrude managed not to giggle, in fact everybody managed not to giggle; they were probably an unusually healthy group from the mental point of view. They were also given a little written test with such questions as "What is a window?" A laughably easy test, all in all.

Then they were led into a little auditorium where who should appear but August Spragg himself to give a speech about the war effort. Gertrude was so afraid that somehow he'd recognize her as Earl's wife and order special favors for her that she scrunched down in her seat to hide from him.

There were movies of airplanes flying and August Spragg said, "Think where the boys in those planes will be if you don't do a good job! You will be making engine valves. You are not to tell this to anyone. There are spies all around, all around. What this plant makes is Top Secret. Talking about it is treason, ladies and gentlemen. I tell you that in all solemnity. *Treason*. Remember."

August Spragg stepped down and the Recreation Director began to talk. "We publish a weekly newspaper called *The Valve*," he said. "You'll be getting it in the mail. If you have any news for it, get in touch with me. We have a basketball team called the Valves. We also have a softball team, called the Valves, in summer. We're having softball tryouts right now, getting ready for what we confidently hope will be another fine season. I urge you all to give our team your wholehearted support, and loyal attendance at the games. For the ladies we have several bowling groups. Mr. Spragg here is generous enough to provide satin shirts with a picture of a valve on them, also the name of the team, such as the Valvettes, the Valvolines, the B-25 Valvolines, the B-17 Valvolines, the Valve Welderettes, the Valve Inspectorettes, to name but a few. Sign up with me if you're interested. We also have an orchestra for each shift, called the Day Shift Valves, the Swing Shift Valves, and the Graveyard Valves respectfully. Anybody that can play a musical instrument are urged to give me their name after I'm through here. You get an hour of working time per day to practice, and then you play at mealtimes. Remember now, just get in touch with me."

The women then went to one room and the men to another. A gray-haired woman in a blue uniform told the women about factory clothing. "No going barefoot in shoes. I or one of the other matrons will be around every day to make sure you're wearing socks, and the protective cap. We do this for your protection. Now, I'm going to issue your uniforms to you. I'm going to ask you to line up over here and file past the cage, and I will hand out your uniforms to you. The cost of these uniforms will be deducted from your first pay. Now, line up, girls, and when you get to the cage, sing out your size. Sing it out loud and clear, girls, I really mean that. Don't be ashamed whatever it is. I want you to sing it out."

Gertrude joined the line and whispered her size. She was given four dark blue uniforms, each consisting of a short-sleeved cotton shirt with buttons around the bottom to hold up the long baggy cotton trousers. Gertrude had never worn trousers and she didn't know if she could stand it. She felt as awful as though she'd been handed two plumey fans and a jewel for her tummy-button and told to get to work. She would have turned and run except that wouldn't have been polite, and it would have made her conspicuous, and anyway she didn't know the way out of this huge building.

"Girls, the secretary's waiting outside with your assignments. I hope you got the shift you wanted, and goodbye."

Gertrude was assigned to the night shift. Graveyard shift, they funnily called it. She would work from eleven at night to seven in the morning, but now it was only noon. She decided to go to the garage and ask Earl to take her home.

* * * * *

She hadn't been in town for so long that she actually got lost walking to Sunup Motors. It was two o'clock before she got there. She felt tired and almost faint with hunger.

Earl was sitting at the desk behind the rail. He had his suitcoat off and his sleeves turned up at the cuffs. His shirt certainly looked nice and white. He had his feet up on the desk and was looking into space, sort of sucking his teeth, which meant he'd just got back from eating. The thought made her even hungrier.

He stood up when he saw her. He was such a gentleman. And he spoke to her so pleasantly: "Hello, Gertrude."

"I've got to get home and eat a little something," she said.

"Well, mind your manners. First say hello to Militant."

That was the funny name he had for Barney's wife, to show he didn't like her. To be loyal, Gertrude tried not to like her either. Her name was Mildred. Gertrude called her Milly. "She's in the shop," Earl said. "Teaching the mechanics their business, as usual."

"Hello, Milly," Gertrude called, standing in the doorway to the shop.

"Well, Trude!" Trude was Barney's name for Gertrude. She loved it when Barney called her silly things, but Milly shouldn't copy him. It wasn't ladylike.

Milly came in wiping her large mannish hands on a blue rag. And even though her backside was pretty far across—nobody else had as much cloth between their hip pockets, Earl always said—she was wearing trousers, calmly. How could she? Earl always said fat people should be forbidden by law to wear trousers, except men of course. Milly wasn't exactly fat—more like *sturdy* or *solid*—but she was who Earl meant. A lot Milly cared. Life must be pretty easy when you go through it like Milly, not caring about being a lady or keeping your hands clean or what anybody thought. She left the restroom door open—Earl rolled his eyes to heaven—and yelled out while scrubbing her hands, "Listen, Owl, those guys are just waiting till I turn my back to fudge on that overhaul. Trude and I are going out for a bite to eat. Don't let them call that job done till it's done."

"I'll be taking *Trude* home and you can look after the *guys* yourself," Earl said. He said Milly's words in a funny voice, to show he wouldn't touch them with anything but tongs or a ten-foot pole, but Milly was too crude to understand.

"Why, she's starving," Milly said. "She's green around the ears. Come on, Trude. I'm hungry too."

Gertrude looked to Earl for permission. "Come on, I'll take you home," he said.

Gertrude smiled and followed Earl. Milly just stood there scratching her head, so to speak. Of course she would, not knowing the first thing about love or what being a wife meant. Sometimes when Earl was drinking, he said Milly wasn't even normal, wasn't even a real woman, had very odd desires, but Gertrude didn't let herself think about that.

At the door, Gertrude couldn't resist turning for just a second and asking, "How's Barney?"

"Having the time of his life," Milly said. "He's a big kid at heart."

"I suppose you worry about him."

"He's got a charmed life. He was born lucky."

"I suppose you miss him."

"Oh, yes and no. I'm glad to get out of making his lunch for a while."

Earl said, "Gertrude, would you rather walk home?" so Gertrude scurried to the car without even taking time to wave goodbye.

It wasn't until they were on the road that he asked about the job, did she get it?

"Oh, yes. I wondered why you didn't ask before."

"Frankly, I'm not overjoyed at having my wife a factory hand. The name Sunup still means *some*thing around here."

"You don't want Milly to know?"

"Frankly, no, I don't."

"Well—well—" but Gertrude could not get the words out. Milly with grease on her hands, coarse language on her lips, trousers on her—legs—indifference in her heart for Barney! too high and mighty, too *Sunuppity*, to have her ears soiled with the news that Gertrude had an honest job! Oh! If Gertrude could have sent a secret ray and given Milly a good kick right then, she would have.

"If you want to pick up a little pin money," Earl said, "why, that's up to you. But let's let it be our little secret."

"I don't say 'lunch' for 'luncheon.' I don't say 'kid' for 'child,' " Gertrude said—too late, as always, after the subject was changed. " 'Big' insead of 'large.' "

"Listen," Earl said, "I hate that ladyloving prevert, but she's put Barney where he is and you could learn a thing or two from her."

"I could learn to say 'lunch' and 'kid' and 'big' and wear trousers, I mean *pants,* if that's how you want me to talk like, and say 'damn' and 'hell' and all them words—oh, I know them too—"

Earl said, "Listen, I hate that aggressive bitch," and Gertrude was contented, as she always was when he said that.

All afternoon she was contented, or almost. The only thing lacking was a way of having Milly find out how Earl felt. Milly couldn't walk around like a queen in disguise if she knew men felt like that about her. If only she could know and be taken down a peg. But Earl was such a gentleman that he would never let on, and Gertrude never had the chance or the nerve. Someday she would get the chance and find the nerve. It would be wonderful. Milly would be popping off in her bigshot way, saying all the things she'd been saying off and on over the years—that Gertrude should do this or that, or shouldn't do this or that—and Gertrude would really let her have it: "Earl says you're an aggressive bitch." Milly wouldn't have a word to say.

* * * * *

Gertrude tried to rest in the evening, but she was too nervous. She knew she owed it to August Spragg to be rested and give full value for all that money, but try as she might she couldn't stay still. The sight of Earl sitting there beside the radio, the noise of the radio, the bickering of the children—she wanted to get away. She started to go out for a walk, but the moment she was outside she realized that without a way to keep track of the time she might stay out too long and be late for work. So she went back into the house, and for lack of anything else to do she decided to stretch out on the bed.

She wouldn't sleep. She never slept. She hadn't slept in years. One nice thing about the job, she could be up and doing at night without bothering anyone. It was really very hard, night after night, year after year, staying still so the rest of the family could sleep, and staring at the darkness, and only sometimes dozing a little but even then so lightly that the birds at dawn always woke her up. The doctor said that lots of people didn't need sleep and that three hours of resting quietly equalled one hour of sleep as far as bodily needs were concerned, and Gertrude guessed that must be right because here she was, alive and well. But even so, the job would be sort of a relief.

> *She was walking with Earl and she saw out of the corner of her eye a pile of trash. There was a dress she had made among that trash, but she pretended not to notice and just walked on with Earl, because he wouldn't like it if she went rummaging through trash. But then Earl walked on and she turned back and picked up the dress. The cloth was still strong and good. All it needed was washing.*

Why, that must have been a dream. She must have dozed off. How funny, with all the noise in the house and feeling so nervous. And such a nice dream.

But it must be late. She got up, seized one of her Spragg uniforms, and rushed to the living room. "We'd better go now," she said.

"We?" Earl said.

"Well, I thought—"

"You mean you expect me to drive you in every night?

And come after you at seven in the morning?"

"Well, I thought—" But the truth was, she hadn't thought at all. How could she have been so thoughtless and selfish?

He said, "By tomorrow night you'd better be in a carpool, or you'll find yourself walking to work."

"Yes, Earl."

"Didn't they ask who needed a carpool?"

"Well, I guess so, but I thought—"

"Well, you go tell them you changed your mind, that you suddenly realize you have a crying need for a carpool."

"Yes, Earl."

She couldn't blame him for being cross with her. She was cross with herself. He muttered and grumbled all the way to town. He was so right. She kept telling him he was right, that she couldn't agree more, but he just kept on anyway. "Think I've got nothing to do but chauffeur you all over the countryside? Inferior creature, too stupid to drive, can't even drive a simple automobile to run a simple errand, have to come whining to me for everything. Stupid inferior creature, stupid woman." And so on, little bits and pieces of sentences, mumbled and grumbled all the way to town. It didn't hurt her feelings, because it was all true. She was stupid and she was inferior, but why should anyone hold that against a woman? And why couldn't he excuse her, as long as she agreed?

She did feel, even though she knew she shouldn't, a little bit sorry for herself right then, but pretty soon she felt much sorrier for Earl. Poor Earl. He did deserve more out of life than she could give him.

They arrived at the main gate of Spragg Enterprises. "Poor Earl," she said, and patted his shoulder shyly.

"You go cringing around like a beagle bitch, but you won't do anything you don't want to any more than a beagle bitch will," he said.

That was not fair. She didn't do *any*thing she wanted to.

And she didn't think he ought to use that word, either, except about Milly. But she kept quiet and smiled shyly.

"You will come get me at seven, won't you, Earl honey?"

"Expect me if you see me," he said.

* * * * *

Everyone was very kind about giving directions, so Gertrude easily found the Ladies' Lounge. It was full of women and girls washing at the huge round free-standing stone sinks, or painting their faces, or changing their clothes out in the open for all to see. They didn't have any modesty at all. They filled Gertrude with shame. She went into a toilet booth and put her uniform on. The uniform felt so cold and unprotecting, so exposing. She felt like the emperor in his make-believe new clothes. She felt like Eve in the Garden after the apple opened Eve's eyes. (That was one place where Eve was right and God was wrong, God forgive the thought.)

Many times Gertrude worked up her nerve to open the door of the booth and go out, but her heart always failed her at the last instant. Then, mysteriously, she heard a woman's voice calling her name: "Sunup? Sunup? Gertrude Sunup? Is Gertrude Sunup in here?"

"Yes," Gertrude squeaked. She opened the door and went out.

"Sunup?" the matron said.

"Yes."

"Your foreman's been waiting outside for twenty minutes. Did you fall in?"

"Oh, no."

"Well, come on now. He's a busy man. He can't stand around the Ladies' Lounge all night. Did you fall in? We wondered, did you fall in?"

"My clothes—" Gertrude said.

"Oh, heavens! Well, I'll put them in a locker for you.

Ask me in the morning. Come on now. Well, Mr. Owen, here's your Sunup."

Mr. Owen said, "Hello, Gertrude. Did you fall in?" He looked very young to be a foreman. "Well, let's go."

Gertrude hugged herself to hide as much of the uniform as possible and followed him. She felt so foolish, so, practically, hysterical. There was a danger that she might begin to giggle, or else cry. She didn't know which. To prevent either one, she began to talk, and the first thing that came into her head was, "Mister says I've got to get a carpool. I live clear out in the country, on River Road, and I don't know who'd be going clear out there but that's what Mister says. This certainly is a large place. A person certainly could get lost awful easy in here."

"Just follow the signs. The aisles are all numbered," Mr. Owen said. He led her past blocks and blocks of machines, which were not black and greasy but almost pretty, gray or light green with whirling silver parts. At last he stopped at what he said was a time clock and showed her where her timecard was and how to punch in. "And right over here on inspection, on the Zyglo Line, is where you'll be working," he said.

She didn't like the looks of it. She had expected to work alone, running a machine, and here she'd have to be with other women. She was afraid of women. Women judged her.

Mr. Owen said, "Here, here's the oiling. You take a crate of valves." He lifted a long greasy black box that had shiny metal toadstools stuck down through holes in the top. Were those valves? The only valves Gertrude knew about were the ones in bike tires. These surprised her, so big and cold and shiny. They were a foot long. You could hammer with them. "This is the stem," Mr. Owen said, pointing. "This is the stem end. This is the head. This little flat border around the head is the seat." Gertrude didn't understand a word he said. "You take these valves and you look at the tag, does it stay 'stem end' or 'seat'?"

"Seat," Gertrude said.

"Good. You're right. It says seat. So then you paint the oil all around the seat like this. Let's see you do it. That's just fine. Then when you've got the whole crateful oiled, you put the crate up here on this conveyor table and get another crate. Got it? Keep the table full. Got it?"

"Yes," Gertrude said.

"The crates move down the table on the rollers, you see, and when they get to this sink here, the girls that are washing, they wash them, they wash the most of the oil off. What they do is, they wash off what oil will come, but if there's any crack or flaw in the valve, the oil stays in that, you see."

"Yes," Gertrude lied.

"Then the next girls in line here, they wipe the valves off, and then the next ones here, they roll the valves in this yellow powder you see here. Then the girl around back here— hi, Persis."

"Hi, Rupe."

"Persis, Gertrude."

Gertrude gave Persis a good looking-at, and saw what Persis probably didn't intend anybody to see, the little network of wrinkles around her eyes and fanning out in front of her ears. Persis was all painted up and dolled up. There were little black blobs on her eyelashes, and she had blue eyelids, and she'd tried to make her lips look full and kissable by drawing halfway to her nose with lipstick, but Gertrude could see the edges of her little thin tight lips as plain as anything under all that red. Persis had coal-black hair, shoulder-length, page-boy, and she had a good figure. There was no denying that or getting out of noticing it. Persis forced people to notice her figure with her woollen slacks, if you could call them that when there wasn't half an inch of slack anywhere to be found in them, and a lacy white blouse that didn't blouse but clung, too, and showed in outline everything she had. She was a fast one, a bad one, you could see that. She didn't even really look at Gertrude or intend to remember her, that was clear, and she sounded so bored and far away when she said, "Hi, Gertrude. We'll have to call you Trudi."

Mr. Owen said, "Persis here, she looks at the valves under this black light here, and wherever the oil stayed in a crack or flaw, you see, it combines with the powder and makes a glow, and she marks it with a grease pencil and we send it back for rewelding. Well, that's all there is to it. Girls, this is Trudi. Ada, Winnie, Leah. Well, Trudi, you start down here with the oiling."

Gertrude oiled. Keeping the table full was no trick at all, because the others were so slow. Gertrude had to keep stopping and waiting for them to take a crate off so she could put another one on. She felt impatient, and a little bit ashamed of herself, too, standing there not working. What would August Spragg think if he came by? Would he realize it wasn't her fault?

She looked down the conveyor table at the other women. They were talking and laughing and smoking. Small wonder they couldn't keep up with Gertrude. They looked careless and immoral, and would have looked worse yet except that Persis outshone them so in flooziness. Gertrude decided to keep her distance from all of them. They looked like people who would make fun of her and hate her. She knew they would. Persis wasn't the only one not wearing the proper uniform. Gertrude knew they'd think she was a fool for wearing such simple modest clothes and for working so hard. She certainly would keep her distance. She hoped she could always oil and never have to work at the table.

But all too soon, one of them came down the line to Gertrude and said, "It's my turn now to oil. You go wash.

When they get back. They're all in the toilet now."

"I'd just as soon keep on oiling," Gertrude said. "I'd rather."

"You can't. It's my favorite job too, away from *them*."

That charmed Gertrude and she looked at the girl. Yes, girl all right—probably not twenty—very plain and pimply without a touch of makeup. Dull plain brown hair in a grandma bun. A sad lonesome girl, sad because lonesome, lonesome because good. Gertrude felt like a mother to her.

"Do you know the Scripture?" the girl asked.

"Oh, yes," Gerturde said, though she was a little shaky on some of it. Earl wasn't a churchgoing man, so Gertrude had sort of slipped away too, but she'd had a good Christian upbringing until she was sixteen.

The girl said, "They hate me, just like they hated the Prophets of Old, because I tell them, I tell them, this war is Armageddon. Oh, it is. There was that earthquake in Lisbon. Ethiopia fell by the sword. The signs are plain. Oh, yes!"

Well, to tell the truth, Gertrude didn't like that kind of talk. She knew she should like it, but it made her nervous. In fact, it made her sick to her stomach.

"I was named Leah, for Jacob's unloved bride. Yes, Leah the Unloved. I've even got weak eyes like Leah of Old. Yes. But I don't have glasses. Do you know why? I give all I have to the Lord, and I can't afford glasses. It won't be long. My eyes will be whole in Heaven, and there won't be long to wait. There was that earthquake in Lisbon. Ethiopia fell by the sword. They mock me now. They'll see, when they cry to the rocks to hide them from judgment and the rocks refuse. Yes!"

All this came out in a blast such as Gertrude couldn't remember the like of, ever. There was something wrong with Leah. Gertrude had known there was the moment she first laid eyes on her. Gertrude believed in religion, but my goodness.

She saw Persis and the rest coming back and scurried to the sink to be ready to work when they were. She stood there waiting, looking back a little to smile at Leah. You don't want to get on the wrong side of crazy people. You never know what they might do.

Persis stood at the black-light box. The other two seated themselves at the table. "Wash away, honey," Ada said. She was waiting to dry.

"Like this?" Gertrude asked.

"Here, I'll show you." Ada took two valves in each tough little tanned hand and swirled them in the bubblingest part of the hot water. She was small and strong. She smelled like tobacco, like a man. "Leah get after you already? Don't worry about her. Rupe keeps her out of here all he can. Gwen's sick tonight, is why Leah's here. Persis sees to it that Rupe keeps that damn Leah out of here."

Gertrude couldn't think of anything to say. She stood there washing the valves and minding her own business. She didn't listen to what the others were saying. They chattered away, but she didn't listen.

"Time for the break," Persis said.

"Come on, Trudi, time for the break," Ada said.

"Oh, no, I'm not tired," Gertrude said.

"Come on. You don't want to stay here with Leah, do you?" the dumpy one named Winnie said.

Ada took the valves out of Gertrude's hands and led her off to the Ladies' Lounge with the others. How did Ada dare do that? How did she know Gertrude would like it? Why wasn't she afraid Gertrude would say, "I'll thank you to please keep your hands off of me!"? It was downright eerie, being understood. Ada was kind of a cocky little thing, all in all. Kind of like a little banty rooster, holding herself so proud, but easy too—confident. Perky little middle-aged face, curly lips, her head in an Aunt Jemima turban to cover the pincurls that even so stuck out here and there along the edge.

Gertrude and Ada passed Mr. Owen and he called, "Trudi!" When she realized he meant her, she almost choked. Wasn't he going to let her rest like everybody else? It wasn't fair. But all he said was, "I've got you a carpool. Your neighbor Art Sweeney, he goes right past your place. He'll pick you up tomorrow night."

"Why, I didn't hardly even *mention* it to you," Gertrude said.

"Think nothing of it," he said, blushing. He was so young and looked so sweet, blushing away, pleased as Punch with himself.

"Rupe don't miss much," Ada said as they walked on. "Persis is real good for him. Takes him in hand."

"Persis and Mr. Owen?"

"Oh, sure. It's funny as hell, really. The foremen aren't supposed to carry on. Supposed to live like preachers. If the front office hears about it, they'll fire Rupe."

"A man in his position!" Gertrude said.

"Something about the very thought of having to be good makes 'em can't wait to be bad, though. Funny as hell. Most of the foremen are at it. They're just like kids—tell 'em no, it puts their mind on it. I've got a foreman on the string myself."

"You mean you and some foreman—"

"I'm still teasing him. I might come around, though. Haven't decided. I'm not crazy about the dirty deed. Don't much care if I never do it again." Gertrude took *that* with a grain of salt. Why did some women brag and lie like that? "Still," Ada said, "it's the price you pay if you want the rest. My husband says I'm the coldest piece of ass in town. He oughta know. Son of a bitch. I only married him to hurt my first husband's feelings. Ask my first husband was I cold."

They lolled around in the Ladies' Lounge for a while and then Persis said, "Time's up, gals. Time to go back."

It was Gertrude's turn to wipe valves then. Ada sat beside

her, rolling the valves in the yellow powder. Leah was washing, but they paid no attention to her.

"You're sure the shy one, Trudi," Ada said. Stupid Ada, didn't know shocked from shy. "How'd you get so shy? Your husband beat you?"

"My husband is a gentleman," Gertrude said.

Persis said, "So's mine, but he beats me anyway, the son of a bitch. I'm gonna divorce him, soon's the war's over and he gets home. I've got a song I sing him: 'Have you heard? I married a turd!' And then he pops me one."

Ada said, "Mine tried it once. Just once. I told him I'd cut his balls off while he was asleep if he tried it again."

Gertrude struggled to hide her shock, but maybe she didn't succeed because Ada changed the subject. "You got any kids, Trudi?"

"Four."

"Whew! I got one, and he's a plenty."

"I had more than that, but they died."

Gertrude felt Ada turn and look at her, but she didn't look back. She just kept on wiping the valves. She felt Ada's hand on her arm and then gone again.

"Oh, gee, honey," Ada said.

"One born dead and five miscarriages," Gertrude said.

"Oh." A long sympathetic silence. "Oh. Well, I guess you know all there is to know then, don't you? About sadness and pain and all."

"I hope there's nothing any worse coming yet to know."

"No, you know it all."

Gertrude tried to think of something to say, to turn aside the tears she felt coming, but she couldn't think of anything and the tears rolled down her cheeks. She kept working and hoped Ada wouldn't notice.

Ada said, "I had a miscarriage once. Not on purpose, either. I was taking a bath and when I got out of the tub all of a sudden there were these big cramps and there the poor little thing was hanging down between my legs in this slimy bag. God, I couldn't look at that bathtub for months. And everybody knew I didn't much want that poor baby to begin with and everybody thought I did it on purpose, and nobody believed me that I didn't."

"I know," Gertrude said.

There wasn't a thing she would hold against Ada, because Ada knew, and she was the only one. Oh, Earl knew—really, secretly, he knew—but he wouldn't admit that he did or that he felt bad too, because he thought it would be bad for Gertrude and make her grieve worse, to have sympathy. He thought the best thing for her was to say that it was all to the good about those poor little babies, and after all, if there was one thing they had plenty of, it was children. Dear Barney always said, "Too bad," but he was a man and how *could* he know, really? Milly—Gertrude could always see the relief in Milly's eyes. Milly always thought about what it would cost her and Barney for the poor relations to have another baby. She never said it, but any fool could see it, and Gertrude wasn't quite a complete fool. The hospital people, especially those hoof-handed nurses, always kept asking Gertrude, over and over, what drug did she take? did she stick something into herself? did she know how dangerous that was? did she know she might not get off so easy next time? why didn't she just have her tubes tied? until Gertrude was hysterical.

But now there was Ada, who knew.

Ada said, "My husband—that was my first husband—he said I shouldn't look at her, the baby I mean. But I don't know, I had to look, and I'm glad I did but maybe he was right, because I can't forget her. I mean, that little face—I keep remembering it—you know? I mean, she was *serious*. I mean, life was no joke with her. I mean, you know, no laughing matter. This little *stern* look she had, you know what I mean? Like if a grownup looked like that, you'd know they were an important person, famous or a saint or somebody. I keep wondering what they did with her. Did they put her in the garbage, that's what I keep wondering. But I was afraid to know so I didn't ask. She was *dignified*."

The tears rolled down Gertrude's face. Ada could smile over adultery and divorce and say filthy words and smoke and paint her face and call Gertrude a childish nickname and do every wrong and wicked thing in the world, without budging the love of her from Gertrude's heart.

* * * * *

Earl was waiting at the gate at seven. She knew he would be and was not surprised at the sight of him there all grumpy and sleepy.

She was bursting—burning—with things to tell him. About Ada and so on, but he said, "Just, please, shut up. It's too early in the morning to talk, for God's sake."

So she shut up, and *he* talked, proving it wasn't too early after all. "I suppose you'll sleep all day now."

"Oh, no, I feel so good. I never felt so good in my *life.*" Thinking it over, she saw how that might hurt his feelings, so she said, "I mean—except—you know—"

"Don't apologize," he said. "I know what you mean. You mean you never felt so *well* in your life."

If he wanted to misunderstand, let him. She felt too good to worry about it.

* * * * *

That night Gertrude heard a car horn out front and assumed it meant Art Sweeney had come to take her to work. It wasn't until she'd gone out and climbed into the car and it had raced away lickety-split through the night that the question crossed her mind: What am I doing here?

Who were these people? Honest Spragg employees going

to work, or three thugs and their Moll, plotting evil against Gertrude? She couldn't see their faces in the dark, or tell anything from their voices except that one man was tongue-tied. Her heart was in her mouth, but she sat very still and didn't let on. She'd feel pretty silly if she made a fuss for nothing.

From her corner of the back seat she studied the driver's profile, which was dimly lit from the dashboard. Was he Art Sweeney, her neighbor? If only she knew her neighbors. She was as bad as her mother, not knowing neighbors. "Let thy foot be seldom in thy neighbor's house," her mother had always said, which was straight out of the Bible and probably good advice too, but it made Gertrude nervous to think she might be like her mother at all or doing like her mother in anything. If she lived through this night, she would make friends with her neighbors. Never again would she study a person and try to guess if he was a neighbor or a thug.

He definitely had a criminal turn of feature, a thuggish look. That heavy jaw! Those thick hands curled on the steering wheel! Nobody who lived on River Road could look like that.

As she watched, he opened his cruel mouth and began to chuckle. "Oh, you don't like my dims, don't you?" he said. He turned to Gertrude. "He don't like my dims."

Gertrude managed to squeak out, "Who?"

"That car that's coming. See, he's giving me his brights. He thinks my dims is brights. Okay, Mister, if you think them's bright, how do you like *this*?" He tromped the floor button and the headlight beams swept up like airport search-lights. The oncoming car cringed aside and Art Sweeney (oh yes, he was Art Sweeney all right) laughed, "Ho ho!" (You don't often hear it like that in real life, somebody actually going, "Ho ho!") "Let that be a lesson to you, Mister!" he yelled. "Yup, Miz Sump, I keep every part of this automobile in A-number-one condition, it's all just like the headlights. I take it to you folks's place. You just ask your sister-in-law what she thinks about Art Sweeney's car. A-number-one, she'll tell you. Say, she's a crackerjack, I'll tell you."

If Gertrude couldn't say something nice about somebody, especially a relative, she didn't say anything at all. There were nice things about Milly, but nothing you'd tell. So Gertrude kept quiet all the rest of the way to Spragg's.

Gwen was back at work, and crazy Leah with her Armageddon was gone. Rupe had Leah off by herself on rough inspection, Ada said happily. Everyone seemed glad to have Gwen back, even though she probably didn't really *deserve* to be welcome as much as Leah did. Gwen was sort of a restaurant-cashier type, very thin and hard. Her throat seemed to have iron ribs under the skin. Her natural eyebrows were shaved off, it looked like, and new ones penciled on higher up, thin black curves. She wore a turban like Ada's, and pretty soon some yellowish strands began to fall out from under it.

Ada and Winnie began to plot, and when Gwen was safely wrapped up in her work, Winnie sneaked up behind her and jerked the turban off. Gwen began to cuss and yell and chase Winnie, but it was just amazing how nimble Winnie was in spite of being so dumpy and heavy-set and not so very young either. She ducked and dodged around like a fly, or else stood still and just when Gwen came bearing down with fire in her eye Winnie would flip the turban over to Ada and the whole chase would start over. Finally Gwen came to her senses enough to stand still. Ada and Winnie stood about five feet apart, tossing the turban back and forth.

"No use now, Gwen," Winnie said. "We know now, what you done. Why, you wasn't sick last night, you was wondering how to face us with your hair dyed."

"I didn't dye it, I didn't!"

"Oh, come on!" Winnie said.

"You might's well tell, Gwen," Ada said.

"I didn't. I put a little Tress Redress—"

Winnie said, "They ought to call that stuff 'Hole in the Snow.' Did you hear about that book, Trudi? 'The Hole in the Snow' by I. P. Standing? Get it?"

Gertrude laughed and laughed and made a mental note of the joke so she could tell Earl. Salesmen need lots of jokes. They used them up faster than clean shirts, and Earl sometimes complained a little because Gertrude never helped him find new ones.

"Yeah, Gwen," Ada said. "Didn't we keep telling you and telling you, keep that damn dog out of your bed?"

"It's not a dye," Gwen said. "It's colorless, and you just dip your comb in it and it restores whatever the original color of your hair was."

Persis said, "If it does that to your hair, I wonder what it does to the poor comb?"

Winnie said, "If your hair originally looked like a dog raised his leg on your head, you're better off gray."

"Why're you all so damn mean to me?" Gwen wailed. "If it's a crime to not want to look sixty when you're thirty-eight, just because some damn nincompoops that don't know nothing think you're old if you're gray! Damn it, Persis, *you* pour *stove* blacking on your hair, and then I have to get tormented if I just use a little Tress Redress. You guys make me so damn mad. Winnie, if you don't give me my turban back, I'll—I'll—"

Winnie said, "Here, dopey."

Gwen tied the cloth around her head. They watched her. Then she began to giggle. "Oh, you damn guys. You should of seen me yesterday. I practically boiled my head in peroxide trying to get that Tress Redress off." She laughed.

Earl had been trying to tell Gertrude for years about the difference between laughing *with* and laughing *at,* and about being a good scout and so on, but she had never understood until just now, maybe because she'd never had a living example right in front of her before. Sure enough, the teasing died down the minute Gwen began to laugh.

"I knew I was in for it all right," Gwen said. "You're real pals, all right."

Ada said, "We won't mention it again."

"Time for a break," Persis said. "Let's go comb our—" and she clapped her hand over her mouth, not to say *hair*. Gwen got as big a kick out of that as anybody else.

After the break, Gertrude sat powdering valves, feeling happy and going over all the things in her mind so she could keep them straight to tell Earl. He would be so pleased with her for having something to tell him.

"Trudi," Gwen said, "you remind me of my mama. You look like you ought to have on a paisley apron and have flour on your hands."

"Trudi's a mama all right. She's got four kids," Ada said. Gertrude was grateful to her for not mentioning the other part.

"Four!" Gwen said. She seemed to be sort of—impressed. It was funny. All her life Gertrude had done these things— had children, worn paisley aprons, had flour on her hands— without impressing anybody much, to speak of, until she more or less gave it up, at least as a full-time thing.

"Four! Boys or girls or what?" Persis said.

"Three girls, and then long afterward a boy," Gertrude said.

"Gawd, I bet you was tickled to get that boy at last," Winnie said.

Oh, yes, she was tickled to get that boy. She made the doctor hold him up so she could see for herself, for sure, and she was so glad she cried. And then, while the doctor was sewing up the rips and joking around, it began to seem impossible again and like a dream.

"Hold him up again!" she said, and they laughed and held the baby up and she looked again. She had begun to think she'd never see that sight. She cried and cried with happiness, and the nurses were very kind and untied her hands so she could wipe the tears away.

"Is he all right?" Gertrude asked, because of the others.

"Oh, he's a dandy," the doctor said.

"Not blue?"

"Gertrude, you *saw*—he's bright red."

"Doctor, about paying you—"

"I'll take that up later with Earl. You've done your part. You just rest now."

Maybe Earl wouldn't mind the expense, since it was a boy. Maybe this time when she was back in bed and the nurse brought the baby and Earl came in all whiskery and tired from waiting and waiting—maybe this time he'd feel that all his wait was worthwhile, and the money well spent. Maybe he'd even get up in the night sometimes when this baby cried. She just couldn't wait to see Earl's face.

She was still crying when he came into the ward. She knew it was from happiness, but she couldn't stop. He looked so tired. Poor man. It was harder for him than her. She could rest now, but he had to go to work after being up all night waiting. He did look pleased, though, even so.

"Well done, Gertrude," he said.

"I made them hold him up *twice*," she said, laughing and crying. She was too worn out to control herself. She held up her arms to Earl and he bent over and she hugged him. She'd have liked a kiss, too, but didn't want to ask because she still had ether on her breath and he hated that smell so. She was proud of him for that—he had to have things nice, he wasn't like some men, an animal—and it didn't hurt her feelings that he wouldn't make an exception just because she'd given him a son. Happiness overcame her and she rolled over and hid her face in the pillow and cried and cried, and pretty soon she heard him go away.

"I guess that was just about the happiest day of my life," Gertrude said. "He's a great big boy now—eight—but I'll never forget that day. Of course, I like my girls too. I wanted the boy for Earl's sake. He was always so disappointed, even if he tried to hide it. I could tell. He'd be so jolly and say he was just like Eddie Cantor with all his girls, or he'd say he was Earl Sunup and his All-Girl Orchestra, but I could tell. I don't know what I did different that time, but there I was with a fine boy. I don't know what I did different."

Ada said, "Hell, it's not the woman makes the difference. It was his doing if you had all them girls, not yours. When those goddamn A-rab kings get rid of their wives for having daughters—why, shit, it's the man that makes the difference. I thought everybody knew *that.* One ball makes boys and the other makes girls. I thought *every*body knew that."

"Really?" Gertrude asked, her heart leaping.

"Ada, you got that arsy-versy," Gwen said. "It's the woman all right. One *ovary* makes boys and one makes girls. I know because I've got this friend that had a cyst and they had to take that ovary out and she can't have nothing but boys now. The doctor told her so."

"Like hell," Ada said. "Everybody knows better than that, except them goddam A-rab kings."

"The doctor *told* her so," Gwen said.

Winnie was trying to get her two cents in. "I'll tell you, I'll tell you," she was saying, but Gwen wouldn't stop and let her.

"I heard the doctor tell her so my*self*," Gwen said, almost crying.

"I'll tell you what *I* think," Winnie said, louder and louder.

"For Chrissake, pipe it down a little," Persis said, leaning around the corner of the black-light box.

"I think it's passion!" Winnie said. The others were quiet by then and she said it so loud that the men in the tool crib heard her and laughed. She blushed.

"Passion?" Ada said.

"I mean," Winnie mumbled, "I think whichever one's most passionate makes their own. Like if the man's most passionate, it's a boy."

"All I know is what the doctor told me," Gwen said, throwing down her valve and beginning to cry.

"And if the woman's most passionate, it's a girl, huh?" Ada said. "How about that, Trudi?"

"Oh, I don't know," Gertrude said. She did know. She knew it was true, except that it didn't explain how they got Earl Junior. But the idea that anybody could tell just by looking at the Sunup girls that it was Gertrude that wanted and wanted and wanted! Wasn't there any way to hide private things? "Oh, I don't think it could be that way," she said. She was such a good actress, from fibbing all through the years to Earl. It wasn't lying, it was fibbing, for his sake, to make things go smoother, and such good practice for keeping private things hidden, because Ada believed her.

"If Trudi says no, it's no," Ada said.

"It's the way the doctor told me. Passion hell!" Gwen said. "Picture Trudi getting girls if it was passion!"

Gertrude was, in a way, hurt by that, but not very much. Mostly relieved. She sat there looking as apronish and flour-handed as possible and the battle passed her by.

"You're all all wet," Persis said. She had a cigarette hanging from her lip and one eye squinted against the smoke. She sure looked tough and brassy. "It's sweet and sour. If you want a boy you douche with sugarwater before, and if you want a girl you douche with vinegar."

"Sweet makes boys? Are you nuts?" Winnie said.

"Yeah, sweet makes boys! Brother, who could doubt it, looking at women? Sour makes girls. Isn't it obvious?"

When Gertrude had to take her hour oiling at the end of the line, she felt so lonesome way down there by herself. She heard the girls laughing and fighting and wanted so much to be there, sharing all that. She liked them. They were awful, of course, and she wouldn't dare tell Earl much about them because he had a low enough opinion of women already. She didn't approve of them one bit, and she wouldn't want her daughters to be taking up with such influences, but goodness how her hour without them dragged, and how all the hours with them raced by. She liked them in spite of herself. Even Persis. Even Winnie. Ada, of course, above all, but even Gwen too. There was no hope that they liked her, but she would keep on liking them anyway, and someday maybe she would get a chance to prove herself the stauchest and most worthwhile friend of all. Maybe she could even, gently, help them to improve.

* * * * *

Going home in the light of day, Gertude had her first good chance to see her carpool neighbors. Art Sweeney, Fritz. A married couple named Orrin and Crystal.

Gertrude looked at Art Sweeney's back. He wore a little golf cap set straight and pulled down so far that there wasn't a wrinkle in the crown, and beneath the cap began bulge upon bulge of red neck, thicker than his head. He turned and smiled a large pink smile at Gertrude. Toothless. Sometimes she thought Earl was a little too fussy about his teeth, but seeing Art Sweeney she could appreciate why.

"We always stop for breakfast on the way home," Art Sweeney said.

Orrin said, "They got real good sweet rolls, right hot from the bakery." At least, Gertrude *thought* that was what he said. It sounded like, "Dey dot weal dood tweet wolls." Gertrude guessed he didn't know how he sounded. He was so cheery and chatty. You'd think anybody tonguetied like that would be a little bit shy about talking, but not Orrin. He went on and on about the sweet rolls. Gertrude tried not to listen. Listening seemed too mean, somehow. But he made her listen, by leaning forward and looking up into her face. He smiled. Toothless too. Not a tooth in his head.

Fritz had his chin down on his chest and was sound asleep. He was so thin and his skin fit him so tight that even with his head down like that he didn't have a double chin.

"Get Fritz woke up. We're almost there," Art Sweeney said.

"Let me sleep," Fritz mumbled, and settled deeper.

But Art and Crystal and Orrin all shouted together, "All out for breakfast!" and Fritz woke up and stumbled after them into the restaurant. They were excited, like children on an adventure. It seemed like a little thing to get so worked up about, but the odd part was that Gertrude was excited too. It *was* an adventure, stopping in the early morning light to eat rolls hot from the bakery. Luckily, she had brought some money from the empty nutmeg can where she kept any coins she found in Earl's pockets when she did the washing.

The waitress said, "They ain't brung the rolls yet. Youse'll have to wait. Youse want coffee?"

Crystal said, "I'll have a big glass of orange juice."

"One large juice," the waitress said. Thanks to Gertrude's experience with Earl, she was probably the only one to understand that Crystal was being corrected for saying "big."

While waiting for the rolls to arrive, the men played the pinball machine. They kept pouring coins into the slot and then shouting and laughing, pounding the machine, picking up the edges and shaking it. The machine dinged and flashed lights. There was a painted hula girl on the scoreboard and she swayed her hips from time to time, according to how well the men played. When they could make her sway, their yells were deafening.

Gertrude and Crystal sat at a table, watching the men. Crystal said, "You don't know what it means to them to not be too poor to do that."

It seemed to Gertrude that they were making sure they'd always be poor, wasting money that way, but she didn't say anything.

Then Orrin's foolish voice rose above the noise for a moment. Crystal looked just plain ashamed. "I expect he sounds funny to you," she said. "I get so used to him I forget."

Gertrude was touched. As long as Crystal knew and didn't blind herself, it didn't seem so bad. Imagine having to settle for Orrin, though—make-do with him, admit to the world that Orrin was the best you could do! Imagine how discouraging that would be. And Crystal *was* discouraged. Her face showed how much she was. Gertrude wanted to say something nice. "He sounds all right," she said. "He sounds like—anybody else."

"His brain's a little clouded, too," Crystal said. "But he's better than nothing. It's not every man that'll marry a divorced woman with three kids. I couldn't afford to be picky, not getting no younger."

Divorce, divorce! Gertrude was sick of the word. Didn't anybody but her and Earl know the meaning of a promise?

But she didn't want to hurt poor Crystal's feelings. "Why, Orrin's just fine," she said, feeling very kind and mellow.

Crystal beamed. "I think so too," she said. "You know, Gert, when Art said we was stopping for Mrs. Sunup and you was going to ride with us, I thought, Oh my God! I thought, why'd Art get us into *this?* I thought you'd be a whole lot different. But, Gert, you're all right. You're just folks, like the rest of us."

Gertrude felt mixed emotions.

Crystal said, "You oughtn't to of kept so to yourself. How was we to know you wasn't some hoity-toity snob? Keeping to yourself and never neighboring! We thought you thought you was too good for us."

"I had so much work to do," Gertrude said.

Orrin's voice rose again, already sounding a shade less foolish. Maybe a person *could* get used to him? Crystal looked almost proud of him. She said, "Sometimes I wisht I had a smart handsome man of the world that could talk right and all, but, you know, Gert, I couldn'tve found a better-hearted husband than Orrin if I'd of looked the world around."

What a beautiful tribute!

The restaurant door opened then and a boy brought in a tray of hot rolls. They smelled so good they almost hurt. The men hurried to the table and the waitress served them.

Fritz said, "I'm a happy man. Good rolls, good coffee, and money to pay for 'em. Nice baby snug asleep at home. Nice wife. She looks so nice, now she's got her teeth." He soaked the edge of his roll in coffee and sucked the soft mess between his gums. He had no teeth, either. Didn't *any* poor-class men have teeth? To think that if Gertrude had married within her own class she might have a toothless husband. How Fritz's sunk-in cheeks did suck in and out while he gummed away at his roll! She almost lost her appetite, but she looked away from Fritz and kept it.

Fritz said, "I used to feel so bad and now I feel so good. I never could do right by my family before, but now I can. I can pay the dentist. He's got my wife's teeth done and mine almost. I used to feel so bad and bawl her out and say her teeth was rotten before she ever married me and it wasn't up to me to do what her folks should've, but now I can do it and I'm glad to."

Fritz made Gertrude uneasy, talking that way. She didn't know why. It was kind of nice of him to feel fond of his wife and all that, but there was something not quite right. She couldn't put her finger on it.

Then Orrin said, "Pinball's fun! I like pinball!" and she knew why Fritz's talk bothered her. Orrin with all his handicaps was more like a real man than Fritz. Manly men said what they liked or didn't like, and maybe even how they changed their minds about liking or disliking something, such as how they began to like stinky cheese after holding back from it for a while; but they never never *never* talked about how their *feelings* changed, in case they had feelings, which Gertrude suspected they didn't. Fritz must have a sissy streak in him.

She kept looking away from Fritz even after he was through with his roll and was merely drinking coffee like an ordinary person. Sissies just didn't bear looking at or thinking on, not even partway sissies.

"That hula girl sure wiggle!" Orrin said. Now there was a man. Nothing sissy about *him*. Crystal sat there looking so pleased with him; even though he couldn't talk plain ("Dat hoowa durr turr wiggoo!") the thought was right. Gertrude remembered again Crystal's beautiful tribute to Orrin and decided to tell Earl about it.

But when she got home there wasn't a chance to tell him for a while because she had to scurry around getting breakfast. Why couldn't Ruby have fixed breakfast? Why not Ione or Tamar or even Earl Junior? When Gertrude was eight, like Earl Junior, she was taking care of seven younger brothers and sisters. When she was sixteen, like Ione, she was married and almost a mother. Would her children sit beside food and starve to death without Gertrude to put it into their mouths?

Would they let poor Earl starve to death?

But Gertrude didn't show how she felt. She just fixed their food and when they were all eating she leaned against the sink and told Earl about Crystal and Orrin. "Crystal said, 'Sometimes I wish I had a smart man of the world that wasn't tonguetied, but I couldn't ever of found a better-hearted husband than Orrin.' Wasn't that sweet?"

Earl and Ione looked at each other like they had a private joke.

Earl said, "I suppose it never crosses Crystal's mind that there's nothing about her that would interest a man of the world. What does she think she has to give? Does she think her precious womanhood is enough all by itself?"

Ruby said, "Yeah, Daddy, if Crystal married a man of the world, that would be a mismatch, like you and Mama."

"Ruby, that will do," Earl said.

"Well, for cat's sake," Ruby said, but weakened and backing down, "any *fool* can see—I only meant—"

"That will *do*," Earl said. And then, after a little pause, "I couldn't have found a better-hearted woman than your mother."

Gertrude was so pleased she couldn't even protest, the way she knew she ought to. She ought to say, "I've got a pretty mean temper," or something modest like that, but she was so choked up she couldn't say a thing.

After everyone had gone to school and work, Gertrude cleaned and washed and ironed and baked, uplifted and happy because Earl appreciated her and was glad he'd chosen her out of all the girls that had wanted to marry him. And Gertrude had had a choice, too; she could have married Clinton. But she was brave enough to choose Earl, even knowing he'd always be a strain to live up to, not easy and folksy like Clinton, the elevator boy in the resort hotel at Saugatuck.

Clinton used to wait for Gertrude at the second floor.

Chambermaids weren't supposed to use the elevator, but Clinton liked her. He used to hover there and go *"Pssst!"* at her. Sometimes she took his ride and sometimes she didn't. He used to kiss her cheek. Sometimes she stood still and sometimes she moved away. "You're so pretty," he used to say.

She climbed the backstairs with a load of sheets. There was Clinton, going, *"Pssst!"*

"The manager can tell from the lights where you are," she said.

"I don't care. Gee, I wish they'd fire me."

She stepped into the gilded cage and he sneaked the door shut. Slowly they rose, like drifting to Heaven.

"Hear about the tycoon?" Clinton asked.

"I don't know. You mean Mr. Sunup?"

"Yeah. What would you do without me? Really, what would you know about what goes on? He got that big boy's grades yesterday. Earl's. Boy, was that a sight. Here comes tycoon up to the desk. Bigshot. Clanking with gold. Opens mail. Opens this and that. Smiles. Stuffs letters in hip pocket. Casual easygoing tycoon. Opens Earl's grades. OOOOH! Purple. I'll clean it up a little, for your ladylike ears. In general, he said something like, 'I told you, I warned you, I told you till I was black in the face, this is it, this is it, NO MORE COLLEGE FOR A DO–NOTHING LIKE YOU.' I got the feeling he meant it. Very amusing. Boy! Everybody heard. The waiters are raising eyebrows and thinking it over when Earl wants to charge a bottle of pop. Miss Nose-in-the-Air won't speak to him. Very very amusing. *She* got the feeling the old man meant it, too. I sure do feel sorry for Earl, ha ha. Who's he going to float down the river in a canoe with now? I'm going to get him, too. I'm going to stop the cage uneven and make him step way up to get in. He's still up there. Watch out for him. He could be waiting for you and jump you. Listen, I'll wait, and if he's there you yell. Listen, I mean it."

"I can take care of myself," Gertrude said.

"I mean it. Yell. Promise?"

"I promise," Gertrude said, with her fingers crossed. She hoped Earl Sunup was there, feeling sad in his room, needing her.

She did Mr. and Mrs. Sunup's room. Then Barney Sunup's. Then, her heart fluttering like a chicken's and her hands shaking (really) she slipped her key into Earl's door. At first she thought he was gone, but then she saw him out on the porch. Each floor of the hotel had its own porch. The hotel was a stack of porches, like a Mississippi riverboat. Earl was standing with his foot on the railing, looking down. He was dressed and smoking a thin little cigar.

"Can I do your room now, Mr. Sunup?" she asked.

"Go ahead."

She stripped the bed and turned the mattress. She was always supposed to turn the mattresses, but she usually didn't. She took as long as she could about it, hoping he'd offer to help her, hoping he was looking at her. She peeked once in a while, but he never was. He was still looking down at the ground and smoking, and she put the clean sheets on and finished up, feeling so sad. Of course he could never get low enough to care for her. Of course.

"Well, goodbye," she said.

"Goodbye," he said. "Gertrude, is it?"

"Yes, Gertrude."

"Goodbye, Gertrude."

She opened the door to leave.

"What does your father do for a living?" he asked.

"He's an iceman. And a coalman in the wintertime."

"Thank you. Ice and coal. Perhaps I *will* turn over a new leaf when I go back to school."

"Oh, are you going back?" Gertrude asked. She could have kicked herself. No wonder her folks kept telling her how tactless and rude she was.

"I take it you heard."

She hung her head.

He said, "Father has made these threats before. Of course I'm going back. He's no more anxious to have me deliver ice and coal than I am."

That shouldn't have hurt Gertrude. He didn't mean to hurt her. No wonder her folks kept telling her she was too touchy.

After that, Earl was always in his room whenever she went in. She felt his eyes following her. In all her life she'd never felt so strange. Maybe she'd never been looked at before? It was a little bit like having to say a piece on Children's Day, but a hundred times stranger even than that. If only she could know he thought she looked nice, it wouldn't be so bad. She felt so careful about her body, carefully held her shoulders back and her tummy in, even while leaning over to make the bed.

"You could be pretty," he said at last. That was the nicest thing anyone had ever said to her, and she didn't believe it—it wouldn't be right to believe it and get vain—but how nice of him to say it.

He never made any improper moves or suggestions. He was always a perfect gentleman. They began to walk along the river together in the evening and would end up sitting among the weeping willow trees at the place where the river emptied into the lake. They sang together. His voice low, hers high. Male and female. She didn't even mind the mosquito bites. Sometimes Earl kissed her, quickly and lightly; underneath he was as shy as Clinton. It was all so sweet and nice, and they did nothing wrong, but everybody thought they did and warned and warned Gertrude.

For instance, Clinton bothered her all the time, saying

that Earl wouldn't look at her if the rich girls hadn't left him like rats. "He's not a sinking ship, he's *sunk*," Clinton said. "That old tycoon's not *ever* going to give in, not while he's got that Barney to pin his hopes on."

And Gertrude's folks were even worse. Her mother said that Earl was after one thing only, and would leave Gertrude in trouble without giving her another thought. But Gertrude didn't let that stop her because she knew how her mother couldn't say a good word for men. Her father said, "He's using you, girl. He's trying to scare the old man," but Gertrude knew she wasn't scary or a danger to anybody and she didn't pay any attention to her father, either.

Even though she ignored everybody except Earl, and lived all day for the evening when she'd be singing with him under the willows again, all the warnings did make a strain and in some ways spoil the loveliness of the courtship, especially since she didn't know until the end that it *was* a courtship, that there would be more than just this one singing summer.

The last of August, the end of summer, the end of singing and happiness, and more love in Gertrude's heart than her tongue could tell or dared hint at. Full of love and tears, she walked beside him down the river path.

"You'll come back?" she asked. "Next summer you'll all come back?"

"I suppose they will, but I won't," Earl said.

"Oh."

"I'll be an iceman somewhere, I guess. The threat doesn't affect Father any. He says, 'Well, Earl, I hope you'll be a good iceman.' I wish to God Mother'd keep her mouth shut. It doesn't do me any good to have a woman plead my cause. The more she tries to help me, the more he's determined to do nothing for me. Naturally. As I keep trying to tell her."

"Oh."

"Just because Barney's a damned *grind*. He'd have to

be an idiot to not get good grades the way he grinds."

"Oh."

"Just because I like a little fun out of life. I'd rather be dead than not have a little fun out of life."

"I think so too," Gertrude said.

"When *I* want a little fun, I'm a playboy and a prodigal and a wastrel. But Barney—you know who's *really* the playboy, don't you?"

"Who?"

"*Barney!*"

"Oh."

"He can have all he wants, but I can be an iceman, for all they care."

"Oh."

"I wonder what they'd do if I said I was going to *marry* you."

That he would even mention marrying her overjoyed Gertrude, but she was heartsick too, wondering if Pa could be right about Earl using her to scare his parents, and the two feelings together mixed her up so much that she began to cry. She didn't want to. She wanted to be a very good friend to Earl and work for his best interests and not bother him with her hurt feelings, but cry she did. No wonder her folks laughed at her and said her kidneys were too close to her eyes. Bawlbaby, they called her, and she certainly was acting like one.

Then Earl noticed her tears and gave her his big white lavender-smelling handkerchief and stood looking away politely while she tried in vain to get herself under control. She wanted to run away somewhere and hide, but she was afraid to, afraid he wouldn't follow her, afraid there wouldn't be one last kiss goodbye if she ran away. So for some minutes they stood there like that, and then without looking at her even yet, he said, "Do you *love* me?"

"Oh, yes, yes, I do," she said.

"You mean, even with no future or anything?"

"Oh, yes."

He turned and put his arms around her. She stretched up and laid her cheek against his throat.

"I'm—amazed," he said. "I can't tell you—I think nobody ever loved me before."

"I'll love you forever and ever and ever."

"Maybe I'll take you up on that. Maybe that's what I need."

He didn't say he loved her. She was glad, because she knew he didn't, and she didn't want him to pretend with her, ever. Someday he would love her. She'd love him so much, and be such a good wife, that he just wouldn't be able to keep himself from it. She would study and learn and get to be good enough for him. She'd learn to dance and play tennis, she'd learn to live in his world. She was young—sixteen—and healthy, and she could be pretty—Earl had said so—and her teachers had always told her she was intelligent and could learn if she wanted to, and now she wanted to, and she would.

Well, not quite everything turned out as intended. She never learned tennis because Earl lost interest in it and after while she got pregnant and kept on being pregnant for a good many years, but who wouldn't rather have babies than play tennis anyway? And there were quite a few things about grammar and manners and like that, that she just couldn't get through her head; but she did work for him, and for his children, and love him without fail, and he must have been quietly appreciating it all through the years or else he wouldn't have shut Ruby up and told her, "I couldn't have found a better-hearted woman than your mother."

* * * * *

It was funny, but when Gertrude was getting dressed for work that night, she felt like looking at herself. She felt like getting up on a chair and looking at her figure in the mirror. With her Spragg uniform on, of course—nothing nasty—but even *so*. It was just too silly, and she wouldn't dream of really doing it, but the silly idea kept cropping up. Funny. And she felt like putting a little dab of Ione's perfume on. She felt like maybe buying a very small bottle of her own, after payday. Too silly to give another thought to. She ran her hands around her middle to make sure everything was buttoned, her mind firmly set on being sensible, and what should come sneaking in but the thought that she had a pretty good body, not necessarily scrawny, maybe just trim and strong instead. Heavens!

For a while she couldn't think what might ail her—after all, leaving home and children and husband to slave all night *should* make her sad—and then she realized it was the nice thing Earl had said that made her so unlike herself. It was a relief, all in all, to know it was that, and that she could still react so to him after all these years, that she really was true blue. And yet, if a few little words of appreciation could go to her head like that, it was no wonder he didn't ordinarily say much. She decided it would be just as well to hide her silliness from him.

She peeked into the living room. Everything was ordinary. Earl was sitting there listening to the radio, digging the earpiece of his glasses into his eyesocket. Around and around and around his eyeball the tip of the earpiece went. Personally she wouldn't have done that, but he liked it.

She felt more sensible already, just from peeking at him like that, but she didn't trust herself to stay sensible, so she waited in the bedroom until she heard Art Sweeney's horn out front, and then she made a dash for the door, calling, "Goodnight, Earl," on the run, without looking at him, and shut the door behind her—just in time, because there was the feeling again. *Cocky. Conceited.* She *swaggered* down the driveway to Art's car. Her legs felt so good, so easy-working. All the way to Spragg's she chattered and giggled with Crystal, and she felt like smiling at the plant protection man at the gate so she did, and she said hello to him, too.

Ada was at the time clock punching in. "Well, hi, Happy," she said. Gertrude wanted to say, "I am, I am, I am!" but she just smiled. She punched in and then they walked over to the Zyglo Line. The swing shift was still working, so they sat down on some crates to wait. Gwen and Winnie and Persis came along pretty soon and sat down with them. Having friends was nice.

Winnie said, "Hey, what's Rupe doing over there?"

From the way Persis stiffened up, Gertrude guessed maybe she really did care about Rupe. Maybe it wasn't all bad, if Persis really was good for him and made a better foreman of him, the way Ada said.

"Over where?" Persis said.

"Over there with the welders."

Yes, there he was, going down the row of welders. He had a little box in his hand. Persis stood up.

Ada said, "I do believe he's passing out cigars, Persis."

"Yeah," Persis said.

"Kind of a funny way to break it to you," Gwen said.

Persis didn't turn around to answer. "Yeah," she said.

The swing shift left. Rupe came over to the Zyglo Line. He was smiling a little sick smile. Earl Junior smiled that way sometimes. "Come on, girls," Rupe said, "get it in gear." He didn't look at Persis.

Winnie said, "Get a baby, Rupe?"

"Sure did!" he said. "Nice big boy. Eight pounds."

Ada said, "Good for you, Rupe."

"Yeah, good for you," everybody said, except Persis.

She said, "I want to see you."

"Well, I'm pretty busy, uh, Persis."

"Forget my name for a minute there? Have kind of a hard time keeping track of everybody?"

"Listen, I've got to see a guy. I'll be back."

"*You* listen!"

"Not here."

"Then where?"

"I'll see you later."

"What makes you think so?"

"Not here, Persey."

"Don't you dare call me that!"

"Honey, I—I got to see a guy."

"Just tell me this—is it yours? Is that baby yours?"

"I don't know. I guess so."

"What do you mean, you don't know?"

"Well, hell, honey, does any guy ever *know?*"

"*Could* it be yours?"

"Maybe."

"Goddamn it, be a man. Yes or no? Yes or no?"

"I guess so."

"Oh, you bastard!"

"Listen, I can explain."

"You promised me—you *promised*—" Her voice broke high on the second "promised" and she rushed off to the restroom.

Rupe stood there for a minute, looking so young and helpless, all pink and downy like a baby duck. He didn't look like *any*body's father, or husband, or lover, or hardly even brother. Son. He looked about right to be a son.

Then he looked around and saw all the welders and the men in the tool crib and of course the Zyglo girls all watching him, and he began to blush. It was amazing that blush, as bright as blood. Gertrude got the feeling that just a little light breeze blowing on his ears or neck would make him bleed. He took a piece of paper out of his pocket and glanced at it and hurried away with a huge, he-man, businesslike, foreman-type stride, but he didn't fool Gertrude, easy to fool as she was, so she doubted if he fooled anybody else either.

Ada said, "I swear to God, sometimes I think adultery don't pay. There's that poor stupid Rupe got himself so balled up he can't get any fun out of either of his women, and he's got a nice kid, and is he glad? I swear to God, it don't pay."

"Poor *Rupe!*" Winnie said. "You sure do pick a funny one to feel sorry for."

Gwen said, "I'm as sorry for that poor baby as anybody."

"Oh, the whole bunch," Ada said. "Whole damn bunch. I don't know who's worst off. I just said Rupe, cause if he only knew it he's got something nice, and the poor stupid nitwit, he don't know it, he thinks there'll be something better later on to feel happy about, like maybe when he retires on his insurance at age sixty-five, that'll be a good day, but the day he gets a big healthy kid, that's a day to feel like hell."

Winnie said, "Well, Persis ain't doing much to help him get the good of it."

Gwen said, "Quiet, here she comes. Take it easy on her. I know you morons. I remember what you done to me the day I just lightly dipped my comb in Tress Redress."

And then Persis was at the black-light box, and even Gertrude felt that somebody should say something, make conversation, but fortunately Ada did so Gertrude didn't have to.

"You know, Gwen," Ada said, "I don't know if it's these old eyes or what, but I think I'm getting used to your hair," and a few more words in that vein, all unnecessary, because Persis was the most cheerful ever. Usually she stuck to her work and didn't say much, but now she stuck her head around the corner of the box and chattered and chattered.

"You none of you said how swell I look tonight," she said. "After all I went through today for it. I went and got me a shampoo and dye-job and set, and the beauty operator,

she said, 'My God, Madam!'—that's me, you didn't know I
was a Madam, I bet. 'My God, Madam,' she says, 'you got too
much hair. When I get it in the sink there's no room for
water.' But I said what my mother always taught me—you
knew I have a mother?—I said, 'Where there's a will there's
a way,' and I wouldn't let her give up. So finally she got all
my hair *wet*, anyway, and she set to with this little teentsy
cup of shampoo—I should've warned her, but I hoped she
knew her business—but at last she faced facts and emptied
this gallon of shampoo on me and got me all sudsed up. And
she worked and tugged and hefted away, and first thing I
knew she was ready to rinse. Well, she rinsed away, with the
hose, you know, and then she stopped and I said, 'Hey,
you're not done,' and she said, 'I can't get no more suds to
wrench down the drain for a while.' So we waited, and she'd
rinse and wait and rinse and wait, and after about half an
hour she had, like they say on the news, the beachhead
secured, and I said, 'Now the blackest dye you've got,' and
she said she'd rather die, but I kept at her, and she lugged
out this huge crock like my mother used to make beer in
during Prohibition, and she mixed up this batch of tarry
stuff and poured it over me. And it ran down my face, and
got stuck in my enlarged pores, especially along my fore-
head—why didn't anybody notice I've got a soft side-bang
tonight?"

"You look real good," Ada said.

"But I been thinking, hell, you know, for the sake of
the war effort and the shampoo shortage and all, why don't
I just whack the whole damn mess off? Do I really have to
be glamorous and gorgeous and all that, I mean, does it
really matter that much? In fact, I been wondering, what if
I went and stuck my head in one of the machines—"

"Time for the break," Ada said.

"It can't be—I haven't worked," Persis said.

"It is, though," Ada said. She had seemed very sour all

through Persis's story, even though everyone else was laughing. Gertrude hated to think it of Ada, but obviously she was jealous because Persis was getting all the attention. Ada stood up and got her purse. "Come on, Persis honey," she said. When Persis didn't turn around, Ada put her arms around Persis and hugged her from behind.

"Damn you, Ada, when I was doing so good," Persis said, and then she turned in Ada's arms and cried. She was much taller than Ada and they looked ridiculous hugging like that. Persis had to bend way down to rest her head on Ada's shoulder, and all in all it was just ridiculous and embarrassing. The men in the tool crib began to whistle, but Persis didn't have sense enough to quit, and Ada just took one arm away from Persis long enough to thumb her nose at them and then she went right on.

"What made me think—?" Persis sobbed.

"There, there."

"Goddamn *idiot* is what I am!"

"But such a nice idiot," Ada said.

And so it went, until Gertrude was so thoroughly disgusted with them and everything they stood for that she went and bought a candy bar out of the machine just to get away from the sight. Ada, of course, was just being kind, and Gertrude didn't object to that except that it showed you didn't have to be anything special for Ada to be kind to you, so what good did that kind of kindness do? Gertrude felt disappointed in Ada, but she saved her real disgust for Persis.

How do you get as self-centered as Persis? How does life *let* you? How do years and years pass without teaching you that you can't have what you want no matter how much you think you want it? Persis acted like a baby. Babies never think of anybody else, and if they feel like wetting their pants they go ahead and do it, and if they're hungry that's the only important thing in the world. They don't say, "I won't cry now because it's the middle of the night and mother's tired and needs her rest." But the years quickly teach them better than that, usually, except Persis. Being grown up and the opposite of a baby means always thinking of others and never of yourself.

It was a hard lesson to learn, how to grow up. Gertrude herself hadn't learned it until she was twenty-one, which seemed pretty late-in-life at the time, but wasn't after all, compared with Persis, who would never be twenty-one again if she lived to be two hundred.

When Gertrude was twenty-one, she and Earl ran a little grocery down South, in Gray Oaks, Florida. They had three babies and another on the way, and Gertrude was a baby, too, in her heart, although in her body she felt very old.

So tired all the time. Legs aching. Bones aching. Breasts like boils, so tender. And even though she had a colored lady named Julia to do the diaper washing and all that, there was still a lot for Gertrude to do with so many young children, and when she didn't feel good it was hard. What made it harder was making so many mistakes at the store that even patient Earl couldn't help getting cross with her, and on top of that she was lonesome and friendless.

Living in Gray Oaks was like being a new kid in a school where everybody knows everybody else and doesn't need you for a friend. Gertrude wasn't used to having friends, exactly, but she was used to being around people who were a little bit pleasant. The Gray Oaks people treated Earl and Gertrude like an army of occupation, like foreclosers on widows and orphans. Earl said he didn't mind, that the ignorant crackers meant nothing whatever to him. Was it his fault they sold out before they knew what their land was worth? Gertrude tried to copy him and not mind either, but she couldn't help herself.

Oh, the long days at the store. Earl said she shouldn't complain. There was, after all, no business to speak of.

What was so hard about just being there? And oh, the long nights when Earl was away, as he so often was, trying to find business opportunities, trying to better himself, and never getting discouraged or believing that it was impossible for a Northerner to better himself in Florida as it was in those days. A lesser man would have given up, but Earl was out night after night after night looking for opportunities. She admired him for it, and tried not to mind being alone, but sometimes when the children were asleep at last and the house was quiet, in spite of knowing better she felt—lonesome. She even missed, of all people, her mother, and all the little brothers and sisters, and had to keep reminding herself that when she was with them she didn't really like them much.

And she felt, also, on those lonely nights, warm, or as Earl in his funny way said it, horny. Earl said she didn't understand—that like all women she was forever cut off from understanding, though it should have been plain enough—that in surrendering to the lusts of women men actually lost a part of themselves, an actual physical substance was taken away from them, while women didn't have to give anything at all, but only take. She could understand that. Of course she could. He was always such a gentleman and he never *said* it was selfish of her to want so much, but she could see it for herself, and she tried to learn to wait.

She certainly was a selfish brat there for a while, and Julia only made her worse, but of course Gertrude didn't realize that at first. All she thought about at first was that she was lonesome and needed kindness. Plenty of people never do get over thinking about what they personally need, and she was no better than the rest at that time. Yes, she selfishly thought only of her own need for kindness, and Julia in her way seemed kind for a while.

She was never very prompt, Julia. She'd come strolling in late half the time, and that would make Gertrude late opening the store, but luckily Earl slept later and didn't know about that. There'd come Julia strolling, half an hour, an hour late. Sometimes she'd bring her own children with her and the house would end up messier instead of better, and Gertrude would have to clean it herself after she got home from the store, so Earl wouldn't find out and make her fire Julia. She just didn't want to fire Julia. There was just something comfortable about her, and the babies loved her. She never seemed to be working—always rocking somebody— but somehow the housework usually got done.

As that fourth pregnancy went along, Gertrude felt worse and worse. All the bones in her pelvis seemed to come apart. In fact, according to the doctor, they did loosen up. They were supposed to. "But are they supposed to feel like they've been run over with a truck?" she asked, and he laughed. He thought she was witty, and she was so pleased about that that she didn't realize until she got home that he hadn't answered.

But the fact was, she could feel, and practically even *hear*, her pelvic bones grinding against each other when she walked, and nobody would believe it except Julia. And there were two spots of pain low in Gertrude's tummy, like ruptures, that went away only if she stayed very quiet on her back with a pillow under her knees. If she got tired, which got to be almost always, the spots of pain would join together and form a big wide blade of pain all the way across her. At first she just went ahead and worked no matter what, but later—beginning at about the seventh month—she gave up. She told herself she couldn't open the store if she had to be whipped or killed for not, and she stayed in bed.

Earl couldn't understand. He didn't like her behavior one bit. She was puzzled, too—the other pregnancies hadn't been like this. She had always felt all right before. And here she was with the fourth one, having such a strangely hard time. Her legs swollen, her ankles puffing out over her shoetops.

Back aching. Tummy splitting. She couldn't blame Earl for thinking she was trying to put one over on him. Everybody knew that having babies got easier and easier, and that Chinese women worked in the fields up until the last minute and then went over behind a rice bush and popped the baby out like a puppy or a calf and cut the cord themselves and that was that—back to work. Gertrude felt so guilty for not being woman enough, and she tried and tried, but for the last two months she just couldn't try any more. With the best intentions in the world, she just couldn't. And poor Earl had to open the store. He hated it so. He wasn't meant for things like that. Dad Sunup never should have expected him to do it.

So Earl opened the store, and Gertrude stayed in bed dozing and dreaming, listening to Julia putter around the house. It was peaceful, "You'd feel better if you'd get up and around," everybody said, and sometimes Gertrude would try but it didn't work. She felt worse. She felt best staying in bed. Even Julia told her to get up sometimes, because Julia was more like the Chinese women and couldn't really understand either how Gertrude felt. The doctor told her. Earl told her. She didn't mind that, because how could a man understand? But when Julia told her, she couldn't help it, she cried.

"You just bring it on yourself, Miss Sunup," Julia said, and Gertrude's heart broke and she didn't know why or what to do or how to hide it and she turned her face so Julia wouldn't see and held her breath and tried to control herself, but she didn't have any *strength* any more. She couldn't stand to turn face down with the baby so big, so the only way she could hide was to grab Earl's pillow and cover her face with it. She took a big bite, a big mouthful of the pillow, and sobbed away quietly and then there was Julia lifting the pillow away and gathering her up and saying, "Don't, honey, don't, don't."

And every morning after that, when Earl was gone and the children were busy in the sandbox or somewhere, Julia could come in and make much of Gertrude a little—tuck her hair behind her ears, give her a hug, say, "How my two babies this morning?" meaning Gertrude and the baby inside. Then Julia would sit on the corner of the bed beside Gertrude's feet and tell her news.

It didn't have to be worldshaking news. It didn't even have to be interesting. For instance, Julia told her a lot about flowers—which ones were budded, which ones were blossoming—and Gertrude at that time didn't care one single bit about flowers, but she racked her brain for questions so she could keep Julia sitting there, telling her.

One day Julia brought some thread and a crochet hook. "You just go out of your mind, you don't get something to do," she said.

Gertrude was all thumbs at first, but Julia was patient with her. "You doing just fine, honey baby, just fine." And her beautiful pink-palmed brown hands would take the thread and hook from Gertrude again. "Now, watch, see here, watch, honey, you almost got it, just watch how I do this part." The warmth of Julia, the smell of her. No wonder Gertrude was all thumbs. Smell of leather, sweat, pomade, perfume, smell like hands that have been committing that sin which God despises, smell of food and baby powder and sun-warmed attics. Gertrude didn't like Julia's smell, and then she liked it, but liking or disliking she couldn't pay close attention to learning to crochet.

But she did learn, of course, and pretty soon she was making so many beautiful things—doilies, pot holders, head-rests for the chairs, open-work sweaters for the children to wear on coolish mornings.

Such happy days, peaceful in bed, crocheting, listening

to Julia sweep or sing or rock the babies at naptime. Creak creak went the rocking chair, until the babies were all asleep, and Gertrude was too.

That's how little it took to make her happy. Maybe, she thought, I'm not unhappy by nature after all, when fifteen minutes a day of having somebody baby me can make me so happy. What she didn't know then was that we are not born to be happy, but to do our duty. She shirked her duties every one, and went aching after happiness, which, to a baby like herself at twenty-one, meant being babied. If only Earl would baby her. If only Earl would give her that fifteen minutes a day. She didn't really want it from Julia. She wanted it from Earl.

She hoped he'd notice the change in her and ask about the cause, but of course he had more important things to do than study out every little thing about her moods. It was childish of her to expect it.

She realized she'd have to mention it herself, and after a while she found the chance. It was evening. The children were playing in their room. Gertrude was on the bed, resting, gathering strength to put the children to bed. Earl was in the bedroom putting on a clean shirt, getting ready to go out. The first shirt he took was all right—no buttons missing, no wrinkles ironed in—so he wasn't forced to lose his temper. The moment seemed perfect for talking about happiness.

"Earl, honey?"

"Umm?"

"Talk to me."

"There's nothing to say."

"Call me 'Baby.'"

"*Baby?*"

"Not like that. Say it like Julia does. Say, 'How's my baby today?'"

"For God's sake, what are you two *up* to?"

"Why, nothing. She gives me a little hug and calls me baby."

"And that's nothing?"

Foolishly, she tried to bluff. "What's wrong with that?"

"What's wrong? If I said Cooper gave me a little hug and called me baby—" Earl's voice went way up high and he wet his finger and smoothed his eyebrow down—"you'd know damned good and well what's wrong with that."

"But—"

"But nothing. You think just because you're a woman you can get away with anything."

"But women don't—do they?"

"Oh, don't they?"

She felt shame so horrible, such waves and waves of horror and shame: O rocks hide me, O earth open and swallow me, O death come now.

Unbearably, he kept talking. Standing beside the bed, tall above her, jingling his keys in his pocket, talking *nicely,* without anger. "I don't care if you take a lover, but pay me the compliment of taking a man, white if possible."

"Oh no, no, I only love you."

"And treat your next servant like a servant. You know it's not necessary to have a servant love you. I suppose you have a natural sympathy for the servant classes, but do me the compliment of remembering you're a Sunup now."

He was as unpitying as a baby being born. Her sobs didn't make him stop. He was so right, and she knew it. She only wished he'd see that he'd said enough, that she understood, that she would end all that, that it was ended already. The thought of Julia made her sick. Earl didn't need to say what she now saw for herself—that Julia was using her, honeying her up to get out of doing a good job, and then, no doubt, going back to her people and laughing. Gertrude didn't doubt for a second that Julia was saying,

"Juss hug Miss Sunup and she don't care if you sweep the floor or not." Gertrude didn't need Earl to tell her, but he wouldn't stop telling her, and he said she was just trying to pull a fast one on him, staying in bed, playing sick.

"You're just trying to make a chronic invalid out of yourself. You have to learn to do what you're supposed to whether you feel like it or not. Do you think I go to that damned store every day because I *want* to? I do my part, and I want you to do yours."

"Yes, Earl."

"Will you fire her or will I?"

If he did it, he'd hurt Julia's feelings. "I will," Gertrude said.

And she did, the very next morning. It was one of the hardest things she'd ever done. She couldn't have done it at all except that she hated the sight of Julia, and the hatred made her feel strong enough to work and work, forever, alone, to death.

"I'm much stronger now and I won't need you now," she said. She couldn't quite forget just yet what Julia had seemed for a while to mean, and that's why she said it that way instead of the way her better self knew she should: "You're lazy and immoral and get out."

Julia was certainly surprised. She didn't say anything for a minute and then she said, "Okay," and went sauntering off, leaving a tub full of diapers. Gertrude had no washing machine because while Julia did the washing it wasn't necessary. Gertrude cried, but Julia was gone by then and didn't know. Gertrude stood over the tub and scrubbed the diapers on the scrub board and rinsed them with her tears.

Earl was right. She wasn't as sick as she thought. If she kept one hand pushed hard against the pain, she could do everything she was supposed to do. Her skin didn't split and let her insides pour out. It was all just her imagination that it was going to. Maybe her work took a lot longer than as if she'd had two hands free, but what did she need to save time for? She couldn't chase the children, but she solved that problem too, by shutting them up in one room and not caring how messy they made it during the day and then cleaning it after they were asleep.

It was not easy, and yet there was a satisfaction in that struggle to grow up. Earl was right. You can do what you know you have to do. Earl certainly made a woman of her. She was grateful. Anything's hard until you face up to it. It was a point of pride with her now not to give in no matter how she felt. She wouldn't care to be soft and pampered like other women. They didn't even deserve the name of women, because they couldn't do what she could. And she couldn't have done it either if it hadn't been for Earl.

Maybe she shouldn't be too hard on Persis after all, Gertrude thought, since not everybody could be lucky enough to have Earl's help in the hard job of growing up.

Even so, there was no harm in merely agreeing when Gwen said, "You know, much as I like Persis, I can't say I'm exactly on her side in all this."

Gwen said it, and all Gertrude said was, "Yes, she's just thinking of herself alone."

Ada said, "Don't everybody think about themselves?"

"*I* don't," Gertrude said. "I think about my husband and children and what *they* want."

"No kidding! I be ding, like Grampa used to say."

So even though it seemed a little wrong to share such a precious private memory with Ada, of all people, who went around hugging Persis of all people, Gertrude's desire to help Ada understand urged her on and she told a little bit about her coming-of-age in Gray Oaks.

Ada really listened, listened absolutely, and that made Gertrude tell a little more than she meant to, more than she should have.

For instance, Ada pried into exactly where the pain was and said, "That's your suspensory ligament. I had that. It's *awful*."

"But thanks to my husband, I saw it through."

"Thanks! I'd have his balls for that day's work," Ada said.

"You don't understand. He did it for my own good."

"Uh huh."

"And I love him all the better for it."

"Hell, you don't love him. You pretend he don't exist."

How could Ada take hold of the wrong end like that and twist the finest thing Gertrude ever did into something mean of Earl's? That was what Ada was really saying: Earl was mean and awful but Gertrude pretended he wasn't so she wouldn't have to think of something else to do with her life. Gertrude's love was just make-believe, Ada was saying.

* * * * *

At first Gertrude was furious at Ada, but she soon realized that everything was her own fault, for trying to help somebody like Ada, who was beyond help. Ada wanted to believe nobody knew how to be married, just because she didn't. The last word somebody like Ada should ever say was *marriage*. Gertrude was above childish temper, even against someone who was trying to tell her that her whole life didn't mean a thing. Gertrude just didn't have to pay any attention. Only the truth hurts.

Yes, it was her own fault. Ada was no better than Milly or anybody else. They were all alike. Ada's so-called friendship had been too short to make Gertrude forget how to go alone. Three nights, was all. You don't forget how to go alone in just three nights.

Gertrude spent the day just being a good wife and good mother, quite calmly, not feeling much except that more and more she deeply pitied poor Ada, poor wrongheaded Ada, poor stunted blighted Ada. And even when Gertrude could hear in memory Ada's awful words, what she felt (so hard she couldn't breathe) was pity.

In the evening she rested. She couldn't sleep. That seemed funny, and she realized that she'd been sleeping fine for three days. All right, in Fool's Paradise you sleep. She didn't need sleep if that was the way to get it.

At least she was wide awake when she punched her time-card, which was more than could be said of Ada. Ada was at the clock, yawning. Gertrude was too proud to try to avoid her.

Ada woke up at the sight of Gertrude. "Honey," she said, "I been feeling my neck all day for what I said."

"You couldn't help it," Gertrude said, full of pity.

"Well, call me bigheaded, but I think I could've helped it. I said to myself all day, 'You damn bitch, going around saying uncalled-for things to people. You don't *have* to do that,' I said to myself."

So this was apology. Gertrude had heard of it. It felt— very sweet. She tried to stay stern, to get more, but it was hopeless: she began to cry, just slightly, enough so she couldn't see plain but not enough to plug her nose, the smallest possible cry, and through it all she smiled.

"There's a pal," Ada said.

"I've been so mad at you all day," Gertrude said.

"Well, sure."

They walked over to the Zyglo Line. "I mean, I had my feelings hurt," Gertrude said.

"Yeah. I got a snotty streak. I go around popping off where it's none of my business, where I don't know any-thing anyway. Hell, *I* don't know what love is."

That perked up Winnie, and Gertrude didn't even mind her butting in. "It's taking care of people, you dumb nut," Winnie said.

"No, you can buy that," Ada said.

"So maybe you can buy love?" Winnie said.

There was enough material there for a good night's talk, but Persis arrived then, looking fierce and cheerful, not at all soggy or puffy or anything appropriate. Sympathy was wasted on some people.

Ada looked her over in a sort of heart-of-gold mean way, like somebody not very mad about it getting ready to ask a little boy how he got chocolate all over his mouth. "You got a new guy already?"

"No, I got the same guy."

Nobody answered. What to say? "That's nice?"

Persis didn't need an answer anyway. "Can't blame a guy for what his goddamn wife does, chrissake. Poor guy's just human, chrissake. Goddamn slob of a wife of his, too goddamn lazy, that's all. Just *lays* there and goes to sleep, chrissake, what do you expect?"

And so on. Gertrude had never heard such vile language before, even from a man. She hung her head and tried not to hear, but how could such a fierce voice so near by not be heard?

And, she couldn't help it, she was curious too. What was Persis talking about? What was Mrs. Owen too lazy to do? Gertrude didn't see how she herself could ask, but nobody else did, and she did, so much, want to know.

"What's Mrs. Owen too lazy to do?" she asked, as quietly as possible.

The others laughed. For a while it looked like they'd only laugh and not answer. They almost made Gertrude angry, until she remembered to laugh too and once again the magic worked, just like when Gwen dyed her hair.

"Douche!" Persis said.

Why couldn't she keep her voice down? If the men in the tool crib didn't hear that, it was a miracle.

"S'matter, Trudi?" Gwen asked.

"She's finding out the facts of life," Winnie said.

"*Now* you find out, hey Trudi? Four kids and at last you know what a little douche would have done for you," Persis said. "No wonder you look sick."

Gertrude could have told them a thing or two, but she wouldn't. She guessed she knew how much good a douche did. If it worked for some people, that only meant that some people weren't very fertile.

"Uh," Ada said, "one question, Perse."

"Oh, I know. I know what you're thinking. Well, she just got him to, that's all. You know damn well a woman can get a man to do anything."

That was an idea you might expect from somebody who believed that douching kept babies away.

"You know how they are, poor saps. I can't blame Rupe. He's just a man. You know how they are. They're slaves to their cocks. Poor guy, he's *weak*."

That proved to Gertrude's satisfaction that Persis didn't care for Rupe at all. To say such a thing about him! Weak! To *think* such a thing about him! That kind of thought had no place in love, and it seemed very unjust of Ada not to doubt for a minute that Persis loved Rupe, and at the same time accuse Gertrude of not loving Earl. At least Gertrude never called Earl weak, or even silently thought that he was weak, even though she had a much better excuse for doing so than ever Persis had.

"Well, I've got to take my hat off to you, Persis," Gwen said. "You haven't got a jealous bone in your body."

"I sincerely hope not," Persis said.

"Hope not?" Gertrude blurted out, so surprised.

"Anybody that's been through it gives it up, I think," Ada said.

"I've been through it," Gertrude said. Should she tell them how jealous she was of Milly? No, better not. About the catalog ladies? That might be all right. "I even get jealous when my husband looks at the ladies' undergarments in the catalog," she said. She hoped it sounded kind of amusing and like a tall tale.

"I really mean, on the receiving end," Ada said.

"Well, I haven't been through that. In fact, if Earl has a fault it's that he's never jealous. I've always wished he would be. Not that I ever gave him cause to be."

"Oh, when they've got the real thing, they don't have to have a cause," Ada said.

"They sure don't," Gwen said. "It don't matter what you do. If you want to go to bed with them, they ask who warmed you up; and if you don't want to, they ask where you're getting it."

"Funny thing, though," Ada said. "Something about knowing they're watching you all the time—keeping watch over the tire tracks in the driveway—counting the rubbers— checking the brands on the cigarette butts in the ashtrays—"

"Yeah!" in a chorus.

"—makes it okay to cheat on them. Know what I mean? Makes it like a game, like, okay, Buddy, if that's how we're going to play it."

"Naw, nothing makes it a game. It just rises up out of nothing and makes you sick and chokes you," Gwen said.

"I still wish—I just kind of somehow do," Gertrude said. "It would just make me feel more like he loved me."

Ada said, "Jealousy's got nothing to do with love. It's just jealousy, in a class by itself. They don't have to love you to be jealous."

"Trudi, you want to make him love you?" Persis asked.

"Oh, he does already. I was just kidding." Gertrude certainly didn't want any advice from Persis, which would no doubt involve unimaginable heathenish practices. Better to be a little bit boring.

Winnie said, "Maybe Trudi don't care to hear, but I do. I'm not doing so hot, to tell the truth."

"Well, it's really very simple. Nothing to it. When you just absolutely don't give one good goddamn about him, he'll be nuts about you. And not one minute before."

"True," Ada said. "Only problem is, then you can't stand it."

"Isn't there any other way?" Winnie asked. "That one don't sound like any fun."

"It ain't, and there ain't," Ada said.

"If I believed that for one minute, I'd go hang myself with a rope!" Gertrude said, her voice trembling.

"You know another way?"

"Why, yes. Daily work, and children, and sharing, and—things like that."

"I remember," Ada said, "how I tried that. Didn't want to mess up two marriages in a row, you know. I might have had to think something was the matter with *me*. Did I ever do the daily work! Waxed the floors every day, would you believe it? And everything else to match. Boy, spic and *span*! Painted the goddamn dining room all by myself, and it took me a week, and he never once came home to paint buckets or brushes around or a mess. Everything out of the way when he got home."

"That's nuts," Gwen said.

"Well, I was standing on the dining room table to paint the ceiling, and I didn't want him to know that. So that wasn't the best example I could've used. But all through that, when I was sweet and pretty and kept everything just so, you know what? He thought, 'Poor shit, poor simple shit, she loves her dishpan.' And then I got ornery and just did what I felt like, and might curl my hair or not, and might get supper or not—and, would you believe it, that man's been crazy about me ever since. In fact, I wouldn't be surprised if he's faithful to me. The only faithful husband in the whole U.S. Army."

Those were the most discouraging words Gertrude ever

heard, she guessed. She felt so confused. She liked Ada, but surely it was wrong to like somebody so awful, so wrong about life.

"Ada," Gertrude said, shaky but driven to say it, "what if young people heard you say a thing like that and didn't want to get married? What would happen to the world?"

"Why, Trudi, you know young people don't believe one thing we say. If there's anything you can count on, it's that kids getting married are gonna think everything will go different for them, than it ever went since the world began."

Gertrude knew there was something wrong with that statement, and with all of Ada's statements, but she couldn't put her finger on it. Ada, by rights, no matter how likable, should be wiped off the face of the earth. She was dangerous, because sometimes there was a small nubbin of truth in some of the things she said.

There was Milly, with Barney snug in her pocket, to prove there was at least a nubbin.

The family had been back North for several years on the night Gertrude was thinking of. It was a cold winter night, very dark and windy with snow piling up. A night to be snug and folded together, but Earl wasn't home.

Gertrude put a scuttleful of coal into the old Florence heater, adjusted the dampers, and then sat down to knit in the wooden rocker, with her feet on the fender. Cozy and nice, but lonesome. She almost, but not quite, wished the children were awake.

And then, in came Barney, hardly knocking, stomping snow. She thought at first that he must have bad news, but he just pulled up another chair, put his feet up on the fender, and smiled his wonderful white smile at her.

She loved that smile. All those white teeth in his lean face. He wasn't handsome like Earl, but he had something as good as handsomeness, something strong and healthy and decent. An honest face, Earl called it, with anger. ("Who ever heard of an honest car dealer?" Earl often said. "Who does Barney think he is, going around looking honest?")

"How are you, Trude?" Barney asked, so tenderly.

As a matter of fact, she'd been crying until he came, but his coming made her fine, so she answered, "Fine," hoping that he'd see the signs of her tears.

He may have, but all he said was, "Got room for a poor man turned out of his house on a winter night?"

"Oh, yes." She could see that she was due to be dull, like always. Dumb and dull. Milly would have thought of a funny answer.

"Milly's got company. Old school friend. On a night like this she makes me go out. 'I'll be quiet,' I said, but no, I had to go out. She's entitled to her privacy, she says."

"Oh." All Gertrude could think of was how strange it was that homeloving people, who only wanted to snuggle up and be cozy, like herself and Barney, should marry people who just hated all that, like Earl and Milly. So naturally all she could *say* was, "Oh."

"Why can't she talk to her friend some other time? I'm really pretty mad."

"I can imagine," Gertrude said, although she couldn't imagine Barney getting mad, even when he ought to.

"I want the companionship of my wife, darn it. What's marriage for, if not to give you companionship? Why should I have to go around lonesome on a night like this? I mean, no offense—I would be lonesome if you hadn't been kind enough—"

"I was wishing somebody would come," she said.

"Look at you there—knitting away for that baby—even with all the bad luck you've had—I hope I'm not putting my foot in it."

"No. I think about that too. Maybe this baby won't need this sweater. But—maybe he will, too."

"Well, to me that's true womanliness."

"Oh!" She choked with pleasure.

"All these babies and all these miscarriages, and you somehow just keep carrying on. Now, Milly—why, her labors were so short and easy, and never a bit of trouble, and you'd think—well—you saw her moping around like an invalid for months on end, feeling sorry for herself. And you saw how we lived, until the garage started doing a little better and I could hire a woman to come in. Toys and diapers and dirty socks all over the house. Pick up a pillow off the couch and there'd be a moldy peanut butter sandwich under it. Well, Trude, I never saw your house anything but just fine, no matter how hard up you were and still are, and no matter how sick you were from miscarriages and things, you've got this true womanliness and you just carry on."

There was nothing to say. She couldn't have been more touched and pleased, and there was nothing to say. She couldn't look at him, and her hands wouldn't work for knitting, so she just sat there for a while. Finally she dared to glance up. He was looking at her. Milly was her friend, and Barney was Earl's brother; Gertrude felt a great responsibility not to look into Barney's eyes.

She said, "Milly was very understanding about how we needed help, even when it meant you couldn't afford to have a woman come in and help her. And she never says anything mean about anybody. She's not all bad."

Wasn't that a kind thing to say, especially under the circumstances when she might have looked at him and brought on a kiss? Why should he get angry?

"Well, I guess she's *not* all bad," he said. "It just so happens she's wonderful. It just so happens I'm crazy about her, darn it."

Despite the anger in his voice, Gertrude didn't reply in kind. In fact, she didn't reply. Here was patient loyalty, like Gertrude's own. Up until then she had liked Milly, no matter what Earl said against her. She had even considered Milly a friend, not caring that she was conceited, messy, and bossy, because sometimes Milly would notice when no one else did that Gertrude was tired or a little blue. Sometimes Milly would be gentle toward Gertrude.

But when Barney said that, Gertrude's ability to oppose Earl and give Milly the benefit of the doubt melted away. Milly didn't love Barney, or take good care of him, or in any way deserve him, but she nevertheless had him snug in her pocket, patient and loyal.

Maybe, come to think of it, Milly wasn't even an example of how men love you once you stop caring. Wasn't she really, on second thought, an example of how if you're educated and clever you can outshine a conscientious woman, the way Mary outshone Martha and pulled the wool over poor Jesus's eyes? That school friend Milly had to talk with that snowy night was, in fact, a college friend, but Barney was too polite to mention college around Gertrude.

Maybe the fact was that you couldn't be interesting if you hadn't gone to college. Still, here was Ada, just as interesting as could be, and Persis was pretty good too if you just thought in terms of whether she could hold your attention. It was very doubtful that Ada or Persis either one had had *much* more school than Gertrude, and yet one thing Gertrude absolutely could not do was hold somebody's attention, especially Earl's.

"I think," Gertrude said very sadly, "that I'm just too dumb to interest my husband very much. Or anybody else, maybe."

"Get it straight, Trudi," Gwen said. "If you was dumb, you wouldn't be on inspection. Remember that test they give you when you first come to work? They pick the smartest from that and put us on inspection."

That certainly was unexpected good news. Gertrude felt

amazingly proud, but also a little guilty—she must have cheated on the test somehow.

"Oh, I'm dumb all right," she said. "Earl's tried to teach me so many things, like how to drive a car and how to talk right. Of course, he's just brilliant. He went to college and he reads *Reader's Digest* and all kinds of boring things. He knows just millions of big words. They have these word tests in *Reader's Digest,* and he knows so many of them and I never know any."

Why did they all look unconvinced? Did they think a dumb woman couldn't have a smart husband?

* * * * *

That morning was Saturday, payday. A girl from the front office came around with a check for everyone. Gertrude's was small because she hadn't worked through a whole pay period, and her uniforms were deducted, too. So it hardly amounted to anything, really, and there wasn't a reason in the world for that check to affect her the way it did. She just couldn't stop looking at it and smiling, and the funniest thing was that the part she liked best was her own name, GERTRUDE SUNUP, written there. She read that over and over, though there's no denying that she looked at the numbers too, and thought of the future with its endless fluttering of checks, and thought of the past with its rummaging in the dirty clothes for stray coins. She didn't feel much like that past woman any more.

She was finding desires she hadn't even known about. For instance, without knowing it, she must have noticed that Rupe had a beautiful ring set with some yellowish stone that was carved with the profile of a knight; she wanted one of those for Earl. And she heard herself actually asking Ada the name of her perfume, with the full determination and ability to get some: à bientôt.

Her mind went on compiling the list and it got pretty long and still grew and the end was nowhere in sight. A reflecting ball for the garden, and an iron flamingo, and a wooden Dutch girl with a watering can, and a little windmill, and a birdbath, and an arbor for roses to curve over, and plants, oh, plants, all the lovely perennials she'd never been able to manage from seed, like delphinium and lupine. And irises in plenty of variety, and lilies the same, and lavender, yes lavender without fail.

Art Sweeney took the carpool to a different restaurant, bigger than the usual one, not nice, but equipped to cash checks. It was a dingy, greasy, smoky, noisy place, with people already drinking beer at seven in the morning and the pinball machines in an uproar.

Crystal, with a pen that was chained to the counter near the cash register, endorsed her check and handed it over to Orrin. He stood in the check-cashing line with Art Sweeney and Fritz. Gertrude and Crystal found a booth and sat down.

"That's nice of Orrin," Gertrude said.

"Will you just kindly tell me what's nice about it?"

"Why, it saves you standing in line."

"Saves me ever seeing my pay, too."

"Oh."

"Well, it's what you have to do. I guess it don't matter. It kills them, you know, to think you make any money. So you got to give it to them like you don't notice what you're doing. And once they get it cashed, they forget where it come from. I know hundreds of girls that do the same thing. You'll have to do it too."

"It's a little different with me," Gertrude said, not wanting to brag, but she really did have to straighten Crystal out. "My husband says it's my own pin money I'm making."

"What you do is, you sign the check and leave it laying where they can pick it up. That way they think it's magic where it come from. It's pretty tough for Orrin, having me hand mine over in public. He might have to break down and buy me a fountain pen so I can sign my check in the Ladies' Lounge. But he bears up pretty good. Him being so dumb helps him forget right away."

Gertrude guessed it was payday making Crystal forget how good-hearted Orrin was. It must be hard for Crystal, to hold for just that little while the power to buy a pink pepperbush, and pretty bedspreads and curtains, and then have it fly away. Probably she had some excuse for talking so mean about her own husband.

"It's their pride," Crystal said. "You just have to handle their pride with kid gloves or uh oh! I don't know what's suppose to happen to *our* pride. I guess we ain't suppose to have none."

"Our pride comes from helping them," Gertrude said, but even as she said the words she could see they weren't quite true. She didn't really, when she came right face to face with it, feel half as proud of how white Earl's shirts were, as she did of her check all safe and snug in her purse, waiting like a seed to blossom into a rug, and crushed stone for the driveway, and a water-heater, and a really good-looking pair of slacks to wear to work.

Crystal said, "Sometimes I wonder if I'd feel better about it if he could talk plain."

"He talks fine," Gertrude said, since saying that had been comforting once before. Crystal hardly heard this time.

"I mean," she said, "maybe if I thought he was better than me it might be okay that he's my master and keeps my pay. And here comes the bigshots. Look at that moron! Orrin the Morrin! Don't you repeat a word I said, Gertrude Sunup!"

"Oh, I wouldn't."

"Hey, Orrin the Morrin," Crystal said, "did the fairies leave lots of nice money under your pillow?"

Luckily, he really was a little stupid; he smiled, not hurt at all, and said, "Wots. Wook!"

"Sometimes I feel a little bad, though," Fritz said as he slid into his seat. "There's the soldiers and all—I feel a little guilty about making all this money, I really do."

"You're just wrong there, Fritz," Art Sweeney said. "We're doing our part. I go into the ration board and I just flash this here plant badge, and they give me all the gas I need without a question. I guess they know if we're doing our part or not."

Fritz said, "Yeah." He just would not be cheerful like Art Sweeney and Orrin. "I tell myself, what the hell, man—you can't have *all* the bad luck in the world. Other folks got to get some too. But why does my first good luck have to come with so much bad for them?"

Art Sweeney said, "It's no reason we got to go because they got to go. You think they'd give me gas and tires, I wasn't doing my part? Cheer up there, man."

"I cheerful," Orrin said, showing the layer of bills in his wallet. Compared with gloomy Fritz, Orrin was a comfort. Even Crystal had to soften toward him.

She leaned her head against him, murmuring, "Give me a dollar, Daddy? Little bigshot Daddy, how about a dollar?"

"Ooh dot to tweet me wight," he said.

"I get my teeth today," Fritz said. "Don't that seem funny, with guys losing their jaws and arms and eyes—don't it seem funny that's how I get my teeth?"

"Tires, battries, all the gas I need. Ask the ration board if you don't think we do our part," Art Sweeney said.

As for Gertrude, she refused to listen. She was thinking sturdily of pretty dishes, and silverware, and pictures for the walls, and a whatnot shelf with figurines and—why, she almost forgot!—white shoes for the girls, and a white suit for Earl Junior.

It was carpool-paying day, though, too, and everybody

except Gertrude paid Art Sweeney two dollars for the week's rides. She didn't have two dollars without cashing her check, and she really couldn't cash it before she'd had a chance to show it to Earl. Even though it was very hard to ask for special favors, having the check to show Earl was important enough to give her the strength, and she promised Art Sweeney she'd pay him first thing next week.

"Kiss that check goodbye before you show it to your husband," Crystal said, out of an understandable ignorance of higher-type men than Orrin.

Still, when Gertrude showed the check to Earl, Crystal's advice almost came back for a second. For one thing, he seemed not to notice any particular beauty in "Gertrude Sunup" written there with the same dignity as "U.S. Post Office" or "Sunup Motors" or "River Road." His whole attention was held by the numbers, and he noticed something Gertrude had not: that her hourly rate was not three dollars at all, but seventy-five cents. Fortunately, she was able to explain that though inspection *paid* less it had more *glory*, but unfortunately he didn't listen and only went on to comment that she had been royally soaked for what, in all honesty, he could only describe as extremely baggy, unimaginably ugly, and at the same time overpoweringly masculine uniforms. Cheaply made, too, jerry-built he might almost say except that abundance and magnitude had never been her particular problems. She didn't follow, but his vocabulary had its usual effect.

"But all these drawbacks," he said, "fade away into the sunset, compared with a certain lack here on the back, up here by the perforations."

Her stupidity made explanation necessary, and clearly it hurt him to explain. "You haven't endorsed it. By that I mean, Child of Nature, that you haven't made your X here."

There really wasn't any way to avoid endorsing the

check, and of course it was best that way anyway because Earl would be in town where he could cash it, and there was no reason to delay now that they'd both had a good look at it. So she wrote her name (that was just a joke about the X) and he slipped the check into his wallet and went away with a sort of cheerful air, a little bit like Orrin.

But that was just a fleeting impression, and very foolish. When she saw Earl's fine strong teeth biting into his food that evening, she marveled that she ever could have thought he had anything in common with toothless Orrin, and the next day when he put on his shirt with the French cuffs and his lovely new suit she almost laughed, thinking how Orrin wouldn't be able to dress up like that for Sunday and even if he did he wouldn't have any place to go.

"I have to see a man on business," Earl said. Would Orrin have to see a man on business? Earl had to every Sunday. Such a complicated world of buying and selling he lived in. She could never have understood it, and that's why he never tried to explain it.

Sometimes his Sunday business took quite a while, though, and they had not yet sat down at the table and spread her money out between them and discussed how best to spend it for the greatest good of the family. There was just a chance that he wouldn't get home in time to do that before Art Sweeney honked out front and it was time to start another week of work.

Art Sweeney would be wanting his money, too.

"Earl, before you go," she began, not feeling shy because for once she had a *right* and was not just a nagging parasite the way he sometimes said but never meant.

But he tapped his foot and jangled the keys in his pocket, and she saw he didn't remember that she had a right.

"I have to have two dollars for Art Sweeney for carpool," she said, very fast before Earl could get away. He was so impatient she thought for a tiny moment he might not give her the money, and the thought of Orrin came again, and once again Earl's difference from Orrin was just remarkable, because she knew Crystal's method of getting money wouldn't have any usefulness at all with Earl.

He gave her the two dollars and left. In her haste, she had forgotten to fib a little and get an extra dollar for coffee and rolls for the week. Definitely she should have told him Art Sweeney charged three dollars. She was just so mad at herself. That's the trouble with being stupid, you can't see ahead and think things through. Her small fund from the nutmeg can was gone. Now where in the world was she going to find fifteen cents a day, since Earl had forgotten that she had a right?

She hadn't been through his trousers for a while; maybe there'd be a few more coins by now. She went to the closet and inhaled the nice smells of good wool and tobacco and after-shave lotion for a while, for the pleasure of it, and then she checked to make sure the children weren't around, and then she started through his suits. A match folder from the bank in the navy blue. Some tobacco crumbs in the brown. In the gray, another match folder that said "The Flamingo." In the tweed, yet another match folder, from a place called "The Red Mill." They almost reminded her of something, but she couldn't remember what. Must be it wasn't worth remembering.

Then on the closet floor, just when she was about to give up, she saw a nickel. It was all right. She would have a cup of coffee and pretend she didn't want a roll.

* * * * *

Gertrude didn't mind about Earl's keeping her money, because she was planning all along to spend it on him anyway. She could see, in fact, that it was quite foolish and selfish of her to think of it as *her* money in the first place. It was *their* money.

So she was not one bit cross with Earl. She certainly was cross with Crystal, though. That first morning when the others were having their awful fattening rolls and fat Crystal was gobbling hers down in a very low-class uncouth way, Gertrude just kept quiet and drank her coffee, and any fool could have seen that she didn't want to discuss anything. Any fool except Crystal, who—with her mouth full, blowing wet crumbs—made quite a few remarks like, "Where's your check, Gert?" and "I told you to kiss it goodbye." Things like that, that Gertrude didn't listen to or answer.

"You thought it was a little different with you Sunups," Crystal said. "Lemme tell you, it's no different with *no*body. Franklin Roosevelt keeps Eleanor's check, if she gets one."

The carpool men sat right there and let Crystal get away with that. Art Sweeney even said, "If you didn't want men should manage the money, you shouldn't've let Eve give Adam that apple," and he laughed his cheery ho ho. The world was set up just right from his point of view.

Crystal yelled, "You know goddamn good and well I wasn't even born yet. I had nothing to do with Eve."

"Oh, you *look* like you was born then," Art Sweeney said. Ho ho. At least when Earl insulted you, he was clever about it. Crystal turned to Orrin for support, but Orrin wasn't following the conversation perfectly, so he just smiled vaguely, like to stay on the safe side.

Gertrude said, "For your information, I gave my husband my paycheck of my own free will, and if the day comes when I don't want to, I'll keep it of my own free will too." And she imagined Earl's face if she did keep her check. She couldn't imagine what he would say because his words were too wonderful to imagine, but she could imagine *how* he would say it and she knew she couldn't bear it. He would make her feel like a worm. In some ways, he took after his father.

Dad Sunup drove down to Gray Oaks to see Earl and Gertrude and especially to see the store. Earl had been too busy to send reports. Gertrude would have but she didn't know how, and anyway she was a little moody because the fourth baby had been born blue and dead.

They weren't expecting Dad Sunup. He just drove up to the store and caught it not looking its best. How he described it, in a very loud voice, was "Nothing but rusty cans and fly shit!"

Earl did his best to explain—Florida humidity, flies, clannishness, prejudice against Northerners, the difficulty of finding suppliers, the hurricane—but he was scared and his voice wasn't working well, and Dad Sunup kept on yelling the whole while so he probably didn't even hear. It seemed strange to be afraid of a father. All fathers yelled and all children ignored them. Maybe if a *rich* father yells, you're scared.

But Dad Sunup wasn't rich any more, and he said over and over that it was Earl's fault. This fine flourishing store had been intended to be the first of a huge chain, a coast-to-coast empire headed by Earl if Earl had had the enterprise or intelligence of a piss-ant.

It was disloyal to Earl to listen to such things, so Gertrude hurried home to clean up the children. When Earl and Dad Sunup drove up, the children ran out looking so cute in their pretty dresses, so blond, squealing, "Grandpa! Grandpa!" in such a happy, loving, welcoming way. Earl caught them one at a time and tossed them up, as naturally as though he did it every day. How could that mean old man resist them? Ione even hugged his leg and gave him a beautiful smile.

"Dad," Earl said, holding a daughter in each arm, "maybe

I don't deserve another chance, but your grandchildren do."

Not even an innocent child could melt that hard old heart. "If you want to make your living with your pecker, you'll have to find somebody else to pay you," Dad Sunup said.

And no he wouldn't stay for dinner, and no he wouldn't stay the night. He looked like he expected to catch a disease in their plain, clean house. At least he couldn't say there were signs of extravagance in it. When he left, he even took the store keys. Of *course* you're afraid of somebody who can take away the keys.

Earl and Gertrude were awake all night, feeling like worms and crying—yes, Earl was crying. It was easier for Gertrude because she'd always been poor and she knew there was always some way to scrape by. She tried to comfort Earl by saying, "It's all right, we won't die," but Earl wanted more out of life than just not dying.

The very next day there was a letter from Barney:

Dear Owl:

I hope this gets to you before Dad does. He made some bad investments in what they're calling the Florida Bubble. Also he played the market on margin and got a bunch of margin calls in a row. So that's about it for the family fortune. When he set off to see you, he wanted to think it was all your fault. It's a general economic condition, so don't let him buffalo you. You know Dad—he always has to blame somebody else and he couldn't get at Herbert Hoover.

I have a farmhouse out on River Road that you're welcome to the use of. It's not much but it could tide you over. Also I could use some help in the garage. Interested?

Milly sends her love. Best to Gertrude and the kids.

Barney

What a lifesaver, what a godsend that letter was. It didn't please Earl entirely—he even lost his temper and said if it hadn't been for Gertrude and *her* brats, he wouldn't have to take charity from that damned do-good saintly Barney—but how could he help feeling relieved? He stopped crying and Gertrude, personally, would have smiled if she hadn't been afraid of making him mad.

Poor proud Earl, always reaching and struggling, always suffering over money. Of course he could have her checks. If that little pin money made him feel better, more like a real Sunup, a little less beaten down, a little more grand, she would give it to him with her whole heart.

* * * * *

That's how she felt on Monday morning, and how she intended to keep on feeling. But it was strange how tired she felt, how she had to force herself to do the laundry and put food on the table, how the children annoyed her. It was even hard to get ready for work Monday night. She hated to think it, but there didn't seem to be much *use* in going to work. The war effort, which should have been plenty of reason, just didn't perk her up. Was she so spoiled and selfish that she couldn't find the energy to help her country except for money?

Tuesday morning Gertrude was hungry. There was more to it than just missing a treat. She was really hungry. The smoky, noisy restaurant made her dizzy and when the rolls came and she couldn't have any, she thought she might faint. If she'd been standing up she would have.

She thought of asking Milly for help. Milly was often generous. She drove Gertrude to the grocery every week. The tulip bulbs had come from Milly, and material for the children's clothes and lots more. She always said things were lying around in the way and would Gertrude take them off her hands, please, but probably that wasn't true. She probably really was generous. Sometimes when Gertrude was jealous of Milly, she forgot Milly's warm, helpless side—but sometimes Gertrude had almost felt that Milly actually loved her.

There was a time when Milly came to see Gertrude a lot. Milly was always gadding around in her roadster and often she ended up asking Gertrude for a cup of tea. She'd hug Gertrude hello and goodbye, and kiss her cheek. Sometimes Gertrude felt that if she turned her mouth toward Milly's, Milly wouldn't mind. Thanks to Earl's guidance in Gray Oaks, Gertrude knew such things could happen and always kept the upper hand—laughable as it was to imagine anyone keeping the upper hand with Milly.

One afternoon when Milly came, Gertrude was nursing Earl Junior. He was so precious, not just for being a boy but for being alive and healthy after all the others. He was a tiny thing then, shorter than her arm, and still so sweet. Milly slouched down in the big chair and watched from under her eyebrows. The silence was only a little embarrassing. Then Milly said, "You're so beautiful."

"All new mothers are beautiful," Gertrude said, amazingly calm considering the leaps her heart was taking.

"Yes, but you, personally, especially." And then Milly said something very strange: "You know, everybody needs that. Not just children. Not just men. Everybody." Gertrude didn't know what she could mean. Who was left except women? She dared not ask.

Another time Gertrude was cleaning house when Milly came. "Don't let me stop you," Milly said. Gertrude felt confident around Milly by then, cute and graceful, and she made a dance out of pretending the featherduster was a magic wand. Milly sat in the same big chair looking the same way out from under her eyebrows. What she said wasn't the same but it was puzzling in the same way: "Nothing but Death's great blinders can turn my eyes from you."

Well, that stage didn't last long. Milly got a new best friend—she never went long without a best friend—which Gertrude was too ignorant and common to be. Gertrude stopped thinking every dust cloud in the road was going to become Milly's roadster. Whatever had been about to happen stopped in the nick of time. What would have become of them?

Milly probably believed that what she had been hinting at was very good—maybe even the best thing she had to offer—and she probably didn't appreciate that Gertrude had kept them both out of a lot of trouble, and that it had been really hard for Gertrude to do that.

Because of course, naturally, Gertrude had been tempted. Now that the danger was seven years in the past, there could be no harm in admitting that to herself. Nursing a baby puts your mind on such things, makes you wonder how it would feel to be held like that with your mouth right there and be looked at with soft eyes—be *adored*—and just stay still, not feeling silly about being adored, and not have a tight muscle anywhere in your body, and doze off so simply. You could envy a *boy* baby especially, because he could move from you to somebody very like you and never have to give anything up. So when your mind is in those tracks and somebody very like you is looking out from under her eyebrows at you, yes, you're tempted.

But if you have an ounce of common sense, you think of

the consequences and hold still until the temptation goes by. Then you thank the Lord above for helping it go by, at the same time hoping the Lord notices you've done a very hard thing and gives you credit.

God willing, the Lord had given Gertrude credit, but there wasn't the ghost of a chance that Milly had. Even though Milly continued to act kind, there was a difference in her. Something became tough in her. The thought of asking her for money for a restaurant breakfast embarrassed Gertrude. She would just have to stay still and wait for the temptation to eat hot rolls to go away.

* * * * *

Things do come in bunches! Here Gertrude's thoughts had just been where they hadn't been in years, and what should the Zyglo Line be buzzing with that night but something in the same vein? Of course there was no comparison, really. Still it was uncanny that just before the graveyard shift went on, somebody was found kissing somebody in the Ladies' Lounge.

The news spread very fast. It was scary how fast. It was a warning against even thinking. At five minutes before eleven, somebody saw four legs instead of two under the door of one of the booths, and at five minutes after eleven everybody at Spragg's knew—even Gertrude.

Even Leah, who never heard anything unless she eavesdropped. She stayed at the Zyglo Line saying, "It's a sign of the times! The Day of Judgment is at hand! Watch and pray!" until Rupe ordered her to get over to Rough Inspection where she belonged. Winnie said, "Lonesome as I am, I'd never stoop so low." Persis said, "It's creepy." Gwen said, "The very thought makes me sick." Gertrude tried to think of something to say too, so they wouldn't suspect her of sympathizing. Since she wasn't clever, she had to make-do with "Terrible!"

Ada said, "What's so terrible? What a bunch of hicks!" Why did she have to turn on *Gertrude*, who had said the least of anybody?

Persis said, "Well, for starters, don't you think it's terrible to crawl under the door and attack a girl that's sitting on the toilet minding her own business?"

"She didn't do that, you nitwit," Ada said. "That was her regular girlfriend. They wanted to sneak a little kiss. Where in hell else was there to go? She's a friend of mine. They're both friends of mine. And you can make what you want to of that."

Winnie said, "Well, you don't need to get huffy. But watch out for them. Queers, they jump you. They're crazy. It's a disease. They can't help it. They need help. They jump you."

Ada hit the metal table with the big B-17 valve she was drying. It made a real racket, and Ada stood up, saying, "It is not a disease. They are not crazy. They do not jump you."

Gwen said, "Ada, if I didn't know better, I'd wonder—"

"Wonder anything you want to. I'm sick of all your pointy little heads."

If you're popular, you can get away with anything. Gertrude certainly wouldn't have had nerve enough to say any of that, but maybe it doesn't take all that much nerve if you're popular.

The Zyglo Line settled down to a good night's talk. "What can a woman do for you you can't do for yourself?" Persis said. They weren't afraid to talk about queerness because Ada talked about it, and everybody knew she was as normal as oatmeal, as normal as school shoes. By morning they had decided that what you do in private is nobody else's business, but kissing in the Ladies' Lounge is dumb.

The whole Zyglo Line was at the time clock waiting for it to click over to seven so they could punch out. Up came that very pair, Those Women, looking just like any other welders. Gertrude wouldn't have known who they were except that Ada kissed their cheeks, saying, "Hi. We decided you were dumb," and smiled. Then Persis kissed their cheeks, saying, "Hi, dummies," and then Winnie did and Gwen did and only Gertrude was left so Gertrude did. The men whistled their heads off, but the Zyglo Line walked Those Women all the way to their car. It was an amazingly cheerful experience, particularly since the men weren't really angry.

When Those Women drove off, Gertrude said goodbye and headed for Art Sweeney's car. Then she felt herself turning around and heard herself calling, "Ada! Ada! Just a minute!" Ada turned and waited. "Ada, can I borrow two dollars?" Gertrude was going to explain why and promise to repay right after next payday, she was going to run on and on about it nervously, but Ada cut her off, saying, "How about three?"

* * * * *

Gertrude didn't enjoy her rolls as much as before because she realized she had got herself into a pickle. Try as she might—make her mind go blank, hum a little tune, pretend Saturday would never come—she couldn't stop realizing it. All her best methods for not being nervous suddenly didn't work. That was scariest of all, like losing the use of a limb. She couldn't stop knowing that Saturday would come, she would cash her own check, Earl would ask where it was, and then—her whole head went plain white inside, but not in the nice way. She enjoyed the nice way. This way gave her diarrhea.

Saturday morning did come. Art Sweeney took the carpool to the large check-cashing restaurant. Crystal endorsed her check and went to wait at a table. The men stood in line at the cash register. Gertrude would never have done this. except that she had to repay Ada. She would save out enough to pay Art Sweeney and Ada and give the rest to Earl.

The cashier took Gertrude's check and handed her a twenty, a ten, a five, and a one. Thirty-six dollars, cash. It was the most money Gertrude had ever touched, and it was hers. Hers. Hers. She had earned it fair and square. She had not whined for it, or prayed for it, or crawled around the closet floor for it. She had worked for it.

Gertrude sat at the table counting the money over and over and smelling it. Crystal was saying something. "What?" Gertrude asked.

"I *said*, are you going to give that to your husband?"

"Over my dead body," Gertrude said, holding the money against her chest.

* * * * *

She was in no hurry to go inside. She took her time, looked the yard over. The tulips were still spelling Sunup— how things do hang on to mock you!—but harder to read because the petals had fallen. The grass needed cutting already. Maybe she'd do that. Mowing would calm her down. She felt somewhat jittery. Yes, quite jittery. Except for being sure Earl was a real gentleman, she would have been very jittery.

Earl came out to the porch. She didn't look at him. He was dressed for town. He seemed glad to see her. She gave him a wave and kept on mowing. In a minute he went over to her purse where she'd left it on the step. She turned the mower around in the middle of a swath to get her back to him and make him disappear.

"All right, where is it?" he yelled. She didn't have to hear him. Then he said it up close. Even the mower ticking its reel against its blade couldn't save her from hearing him then, but she still didn't have to know what he meant and she wasn't going to mention anything he didn't mention. Why put his mind on something he might not think of?

"Stop this damn machine! Where is it?"

She kept still. When he took his hand off the mower handle, she started mowing again.

"Didn't they pay you or what?"

(That was a good idea. Maybe they didn't pay her.)

"Did you lose it?"

(Maybe she lost it, whatever it was.)

"Answer me, damn you!"

Mow mow mow. She looked straight ahead and mowed so fast he had to trot to keep up. His wind wasn't too good. Trotting made his voice a touch whiny and gaspy. "All these years—you've mooched off me—and held me back—and ruined my life—and—finally—you get a chance—to be useful—and this is what you—do!" he whined.

Gertrude became very small, a bird, and watched from above. She saw a shabby but virtuous chambermaid/mother/war worker with a handsome, well-dressed gentleman trotting beside her and begging for money. He was so weak. So almost pitiful. She almost laughed to think she'd been afraid of him.

"They didn't pay me. I lost it. It's in a safe place," she said. (It was between her breasts where he would never dream of touching her.)

"Listen, bitch," he said, "don't get snotty with me." Snot was a word he would not allow, even for the actual stuff, and here he was saying it, and then absolutely amazing her by twisting her arm up behind her and reaching over her shoulder and into the front of her plain modest blue uniform blouse and taking her money. *Then* she remembered that is where all women hide everything. The first natural bank, Ada called it. Gertrude hadn't even made it hard for him. It was all over in less than a breath. She was breathless, but at least back to earth and paying attention. He seemd to be his old self again, like nothing had happened.

"Let's see," he said, "you'll need to pay your carpool," and he peeled off two ones and held them out to her like a kindly millionaire whose heart has been touched by a beggar. "Didn't your mother teach you to say thank you?" he asked.

From long experience, she knew this was not just a piece of sarcastic snottiness. He had already forgotten. She knew from long experience that he had forgotten ahead of time which one was the beggar.

Barney's offer of a house and a job was a great relief, but there were hundreds of miles to go to get to them, and the Gray Oaks house to empty. At least Dad Sunup had in his own way closed the store. Gertrude was trying to pack but not making much headway, what with crying all the time and the children to be chased and Earl in bed with the covers over his head.

Everything was so awful. The children were crazy. They just kept yelling and running around. Gertrude understood perfectly—they were making their heads go white inside—but she still couldn't stand them. Just when she was thinking of locking them up like she did when she was pregnant, Julia came over. They ran to Julia like you're supposed to run to your mother. "Thought you might have your hands full," Julia said.

Gertrude just cried.

"Kids, you want to come to my house?" Julia said.

"Julia, I can't pay you."

"I'll just run them in with mine. No trouble." And off they all went. It wasn't just once, either. Julia took the children day after day.

Gertrude expected to stop crying then, but she didn't. Her hands were still full, because Earl said he had too much pride and dignity to ask for boxes from the enemy storekeeper. Earl was a fine example of pride and dignity, blubbering away like that. "No," he blubbered from under the covers, "I am not going to crawl to the man who brought down ruin on my poor dad's gray head. I wouldn't give him the *satisfaction*."

Earl must have known perfectly well that no little Gray Oaks grocer had anything to do with the Wall Street Crash or what happened to that mean old man's head. This whole boo-hoo was just something Earl cooked up to get out of helping with the packing. And he brooded under the covers, claiming that the enemy grocer had lied about him, had told people Earl's cans of peas had more water than peas in them, while she made more trips than she could count to the enemy's store to carry home boxes four at a time in her hands.

So imagine how she felt when she heard a terrible roar and looked out to see Barney jumping down from the running-board of a poor old rattletrap black truck, front end Model T, back end porch. "Earl, it's your brother!" she called. That made Earl hit the floor fast, but only to go have diarrhea. Gertrude ran out to the truck.

It was some sweet chariot. Barney was some godsend. Where everything had been impossible, it became all right and sometimes even fun. It stopped mattering that Earl was no damn good. There were hours at a time when Gertrude could remember that she wasn't a worn-out old woman, but twenty-one, fresh and strong.

The secret of packing, Barney said, was to get enough boxes and then pretend you're a plague of locusts sweeping all before you. Everything. You don't wander around for an hour with a dish in your hand, looking for the perfect space in the perfect box. "Like some people," he said with a nice smile. "That is Terminal Moving Paralysis, soon to be named Sunup's Disease in honor of the one who first recognized and described it."

And the boxes got filled and closed and loaded on the

truck, along with what furniture there was room for. The rest Gertrude gave to Julia, who said, "Oh, Miss Sunup, I always felt so sorry for you." It's a funny feeling to have a colored lady feel sorry for you, but Gertrude would have hugged her goodbye anyway except she wasn't sure Julia would like it, and anyway what would Earl have said?

Actually, he wouldn't have known. He didn't get up until Barney and Gertrude came to take the bed apart.

The family piled into the Studebaker. Barney drove the truck, looking, Earl said, like a poor-white-trash share-cropper, a real embarrassment. Earl was so ashamed of that truck that he wouldn't stay near it even on the highway, where nobody would see except strangers. He actually cared more about what strangers would think than about what his own brother would think. Even when he was sharing the picnics Barney fixed along the road, Earl acted like a millionaire who somehow had a beggar he couldn't shake. He pulled his hat down low when a car went by.

Beggar or not, Earl had her money and she had a debt to Ada and a week without hot rolls to live through before another payday. That was just as discouraging as being a beggar herself, especially since another payday might be the same. What was to keep everything from happening again?

And she would have to make an excuse to Ada without telling her the real excuse, and Ada would be nice, but why should she *have* to be nice? Why shouldn't she just have her money paid back and be nice in her regular way?

* * * * *

By Sunday night, Gertrude had decided to tell Ada the money had been spent on a doctor for the children. It was wrong to talk to outsiders about family problems, and people always understand about doctors. The details kept pouring up out of nowhere. Earl Junior, say, broke his arm. He was walking the porch rail and fell off, lit wrong, sickening crack, heartbreaking cry. Earl picked him up. Little arm limp as a rag, bent backward. Right arm. Saturday around three. The doctor playing golf, grouchy. Yes, that would do. She could see it all.

But what she said was "Ada! Ada! Earl took my money!" Where did that big blurt come from, right in front of everybody? What about Earl Junior's arm? "I can't pay you."

"He what?"

"He reached down my front and took it."

"Son of a bitch," Ada said in a "good-grief" voice, not calling Earl a name even though she should have.

"I cashed my check myself so I'd have it for you, and the son of a bitch took it." Oh, that felt good. "My carpool says they all do it. Is that true? Do they?"

Gertrude bet nobody took anything away from Persis.

But Persis said, "Sure, if you're dumb enough to let 'em know you have it. What you need is tips. Then they don't know how much and you get to keep some."

Gwen said, "You need to get 'em crazy about you so they're scared to make you mad. I always meant to try that."

Winnie said, "You need to have fits and cry a lot so they're scared to have a scene. They hate scenes."

Ada said, "You need to have them out of town."

At least they didn't claim they'd never heard of such a thing, but aside from that they were no help. Earl would have been so mad if he'd known they were laughing about him all night, that Gertrude had told a family thing. A *Sunup* family thing. With every burst of laughter, Gertrude felt a little guilty, but mostly glad, like she was getting back at him. Still, she'd have liked some good ideas.

"I've got a real problem," Gertrude said, "and you guys just kid around about it."

Ada said, "Okay, I'll be serious. If all their money goes for the family, why shouldn't ours?"

Was that fair? Gertrude could have cried. Her voice got squeaky. "He spends it at the Flamingo and the Red Mill, that's why. If it was for the family, would I care? I want to *keep* it for the family. I want to buy my girls some white shoes."

"The Flamingo?" Persis said, with a look of deep thought. "Do they ever call him Sonny?"

"I don't know. I'm sorry I said anything—forget I said anything—I just made it up—I was fibbing—I just said Flamingo because I want one for the yard—it just popped into my head. I made it up."

Ada said, "They've got cute stuff for yards. I want a birdbath."

* * * * *

Saturday morning Gertrude cashed her check at the big smoky restaurant and put all the money except what she needed for coffee and a roll into her purse. She paid Art Sweeney.

Earl was waiting for her on the porch.

She said, "Sonny, I've decided that if you take my money again, I'm going to tell Milly."

"Keep your damn pin money," Earl said.

BOOK TWO: MILLY

Milly was at Trude's to take her grocery shopping. Seeing Trude had been easy for a long time now, ever since Lil came along and took care of all that for Milly. Ever since Lil, Milly had been able to go to Trude's place and just enjoy it—the flowers loud with bees, the silly doilies, the smell of good things cooking, the cleanliness and order, the beautiful children, everything rooted in that wonderful female energy Trude never seemed to run out of, that she simply spun and spun out of her body like a spider, like the sun. Before Lil, the purest of Milly's wishes had been to be reborn as Trude's child, and grow up in the shelter of her skirt.

Earl, of course, would have had to be murdered.

Before Lil, Trude's place had been a blow to the throat. Milly gave the screen door a rattle.

"Come in. I'll just be a minute," Trude called, not ready, for the first time ever. Had she been sleeping?

There were crumbs around the table. On the couch was unsorted laundry heaped so high it was about to spill over the tall arms.

Out of the bedroom came Trude, wearing lineny tan slacks, displaying a neat, soft rump, laughing at Milly's surprise. "Earl didn't want you to know, but who cares? I got a job. And you don't have to pay for our groceries any more."

The groceries were bought on credit. Trude was supposed to think Earl paid the bill.

"How did you figure that out?" Milly asked.

"I always knew."

At the store Trude bought so much bread you'd have thought she was getting ready to fake the Miracle of the Loaves and Fishes. No careful list, nothing for salmon loaf, stew, meatloaf, goulash, chili, casseroles, corned beef and cabbage, but quantities of baloney and a huge jar of mustard.

The grocer was tightlipped. Milly and Trude were supposed to be ashamed, so they waited until they had the brown bags lined up across the back seat. Then they doubled over laughing.

But all the while, Milly wondered why she was laughing at the grocer for disapproving when she did too. Maybe not as much, but, yes, there was a pang for Milly in this new unbiddable, above-it-all Trude.

I never wanted to rescue her, Milly realized. I just wanted her to do for me what she did for Earl. It's true I would have done the same right back at her, and I would have loved and admired her, but I would have kept her right there cooking, ironing, sewing, cleaning, serving, piteous and wonderful.

The surprises weren't over. Trude said, "Can I drive?"

"Do you know how?"

"You'd have to show me."

"Not here. You've got no learner's permit."

But later, on dusty summer backroads, Trude learned to drive. "Picture an X," Milly said. "Inside it's an X. Push the clutch in. First gear is down here. Second is up and across like this. That's right."

"Earl didn't tell me there was an X," Trude said. "I couldn't tell what he was doing."

"Earl needs somebody to be smarter than. He elected you. He trained you."

"Yes, he's a son of a bitch," Trude said, no fuss, common knowledge.

Then Trude said what, except for Lil, would have meant sure-fire misery: "Wait till Barney sees me driving."

The first time Milly understood that Trude loved Barney better than her was two nights after Barney left for the Navy. Milly was at Trude's watching her iron. The sizzle, the thumps, the creaking ironing board, the smell of hot cloth, Trude's strong arms, skillful hands, had always made Milly very close to perfectly happy.

Then Earl, who should have been out doing his tomcat pub-crawling as usual, unkindly chose to come home. He brought the makings of martinis and produced some excellent ones, which he served in quick succession in beautiful crystal that he kept on a high shelf, each piece in a little cloth bag in a box with padded compartments. His only Sunup Family treasure. Milly almost liked him for the way he touched those glasses. She had never seen him love anything before.

"My wife is very strange," Earl said, hostlike, conversational. "What would you think of someone who sits up in bed and screams when her husband comes home?"

"When was that?" Milly asked.

"Thursday," Trude said, still ironing. The day Barney left. Trude must have wanted her to piece that together, and maybe Earl did too.

Up until that moment, Milly had known absolutely that, timid or not, incapable of making such an unheard-of choice or not, Trude loved her, loved her best in the world, loved her forever. Milly's mouth began to shake and then the right corner lifted by itself, pushed her cheek up, half closed her eye. She stood up to leave, but Earl was approaching with the martini pitcher. "Don't mind if I do," she said. At all costs, Earl must not see that she loved Trude.

She forced the left corner of her mouth up to make it symmetrical, hoping to approximate a smile, and drank and smiled that way and chattered until Earl said, "I'm taking you home," though he was no more fit to drive than she was.

He asked, "Barney leave you any rubbers?" and she walked like a machine past the sleeping babysitter and got one. Earl was waiting in the back yard. One kiss. So much for foreplay. Milly liked to be good at whatever she did, and that included sex. Even with, for God's sake, *Earl*, she intended to do it well, but when she reached to caress his prick he backed his hips away, saying, "It's there." She never did feel it, then or later, with her hand or any other part. She thought he must have lost his erection and moved her body to restore it. He said, "I already did it."

"What!" she cried, her interest in doing well vanished. My God, her movements could have pulled the condom off, there could be semen in her. She pushed him away, ran into the house, washed, praying not to be pregnant, called a taxi for the babysitter, and passed out drunk.

Wasn't being drunk supposed to protect you from memories of a certain magnitude of shame? She woke remembering everything in the brightest detail and retching downward. Could revulsion alone cause abortion? No, there'd be many fewer children on earth if that were possible.

There was mystery mixed with the embarrassment. For one thing, she had always assumed that she wouldn't do while drunk what she hadn't at least been tempted to do while sober. Then there was Earl's tiny, imperceptible ejaculation. Why did he run around? You'd think a man of such puny sexuality would be meticulously monogamous, to keep the embarrassment of it at home; adultery took on a whole new aspect. In no way did Earl's laughable little come resemble Barney's grand-mal seizures, but it did explain why Trude had never got enough of Earl: one can be the mother of multitudes while still unpenetrated. To her astonishment, Milly herself was horny, a truly primary mystery, so puzzling that she looked up "gin" in Britannica to see if it contained an aphrodisiac. Britannica didn't seem to know.

A few days later she woke awash in menstrual blood. With the pregnancy anxiety ended, she could manage the remaining scraps of guilt and shame. They didn't amount to much compared with the anxiety. But why had she put herself through such abysmal grubbiness to hide from Earl that she loved Trude? Why hadn't she seen in time that she could have pretended her face was twisting because Barney had gone to war?

Trude loved to drive. Only the gas shortage held her down. For starting so late, she got pretty good at it. You can always tell a first-generation driver, but she learned to keep her eyes on the road no matter what. When she let a bee fly into the car and sting her without being distracted, Milly declared her ready for a license. "Wait till Barney sees this," Trude said, but Milly didn't care. She had Lil.

* * * * *

What a sweet thing it was to come home to dinner. There it was, like magic. One advantage of being a woman was understanding what it took to make a meal. The nicest man in the world (Barney) might be grouchy if it wasn't ready, but not moved to tears if it was. After all, dinner was just a job. He might even take an aesthetic position, finding one food more tiresome or more delicious than another. He might think children just naturally washed their hands and faces and sat prettily at table. Barney hadn't understood about meals until Milly was fed up. Then he'd have been grateful for anything, but he couldn't have it.

Milly kept being afraid Lil would get fed up too, and was touched again and again when still for one more day she wasn't yet. "How good!" Milly would say. "How delicious!" and Lil, pleased, would make a dimple and say, "You're a nut."

And the kids washed the dishes. That was Lil's doing, too. She explained that dishes were washed in the Navy, right where their Dad was, by command of something called a Duty Roster.

"*This* is a Duty Roster," Lil said, drawing serious official columns with a straight-edge, while the kids crowded up and watched. "Monday Rusty clears the table and sweeps the dining room floor, Murray washes the dishes and puts them into the drainer, and Betty takes the garbage out. Tuesday Murray clears the table and sweeps, Betty washes the dishes, and Rusty takes the garbage out. Wednesday . . ."

Fat chance, Milly thought. I bet, Milly thought. But they did it. Every evening they read the roster with howls of disgust ("Oh, no, not *garbage!*") and obeyed it. "That's my brave sailors," Lil said.

"Why doesn't the Duty Roster tell Jack to do something?" Betty asked. Jack was Lil's toddler son.

"He's just a boot. But you're right. He can crawl under the beds and get the dust out."

"Then put him on the Duty Roster," Murray said, and Lil did.

Sometimes when the pans were too dismaying, Milly finished them. The vital thing was to keep the crew from mutiny and the cook from getting fed up. Cooking wasn't so bad if you didn't have to clean up after it. Sometimes it was even a pleasure.

And how sweet the evenings were, working with Lil in the yard. Before Lil, being close to the earth, pulling weeds, planting, had been all that could make Milly even a little calm. With Lil, she was entirely calm. The clean, geranium smell of the earth, the kids playing hide-and-seek in the long summer twilight, and Lil's straight, shining, russet hair—what more could there be? Milly always knew, as from a little cool wind on her skin, where Lil was, and saw her hair without looking.

In winter or on rainy evenings, Milly read aloud while Lil mended or drew or ironed. Yes, darling Lil ironed, just like Trude. Sometimes Lil read to Milly while Milly fixed a bike or the toaster or put new washers into the faucets. Lil was intelligent but uninformed. She was someone new to tell old stories to. When Lil laughed at Mark Twain's jokes, Milly felt as proud as though they were her own. And if sometimes the kids wanted to curl up against who-ever was reading and listen, that was okay too. There was room for everybody in the utter bounty and beauty of this love, such a sense of no-hurry, time for everything. Love was the warm sea they swam in. Or floated? Yes, it was more like floating. The lady who hadn't been able to stand staying home couldn't stand to go out.

" 'How have you come to me?' " Milly sometimes asked,

but Lil, who didn't like to repeat herself and who did not believe in answering questions you know the answers to, or to which there are no answers, hardly ever answered. Admire Gary Cooper and see what happens.

Milly really would have liked to hear, over and over: Once upon a time there was a beautiful young queen who had a baby prince, very heartwarming but unmistakably a baby, with all that meant. Before the prince's fine young father had time to find out what he might become, he went to war and died. The queen went back to her parents. She picked up each memory and hope and looked at it from all sides and wept for it and said goodbye to it, and one morning she woke up knowing the time had come to do something else. It was time to take charge of herself and her child, because if you don't take care of yourself other people will, and you will not like the way they do it. You will not like the way they raise your child, either.

She looked through the want ads for an apartment, something her widow's humble pension could pay for, and found instead (this is where it gets exciting)

Wtd liv in hskpr chld ok.

Well, why not? You can always say no. She was certainly going to say no. Then there was this big messy house and this big messy crazy young woman, a frazzled juggler who couldn't keep even one ball in the air, a wader who was in over her head, and the queen said yes.

"When I saw you sweeping that ugly gray rug with a broom, I knew I had to help you," Lil said.

Milly almost couldn't admit that the broom was because she was too lazy to get out the vacuum cleaner, that she had chosen the rug herself, and that it wasn't gray originally.

It was strange to have somebody want to help you instead of bring you down a peg, or make you face reality, or knock some of the snot out of you, or make you count your blessings, or give you your comeuppance. Even though it was very close to being loved for being pitiful, it was a nice change. And it turned out to be a perfectly good place to start.

"Tell me, tell me again, how it started. Which one first got up the nerve to hold out her hand?"

"You know," Lil said.

Of course Milly knew, but she wanted the other side of it, herself as mystery, unpredictable. "*Tell* me!"

"There you are in your shabby old slacks held up with a safety pin and a torn shirt and barefooted, and you're ordering cottage cheese from the milkman, saying, 'I prefer large-curd if you have it,' exactly the way Eleanor Roosevelt would say it."

Ah.

"There you are playing *Aida* on the Victrola. You're following the translation in a white book, and crying."

"More."

"You took a worn-out tube out of the radio and carried it around in your hip pocket. You said it just wanted to go for a ride. And you put it back into the radio, and it worked."

"More."

"Betty came in with a skinned knee and you fixed it and held her. You said, 'It really hurts. I know it really hurts.' Everybody else says, 'Don't be a baby. *That* doesn't hurt.' I always said that too. You said kids don't need relief, they need acknowledgement. So I learned something."

And then? And then?

"Betty was showing off to make Jack laugh, and he was laughing big belly laughs and you quoted something really nice: 'Our tiny human April, like the earth's, pours green.' You said poetry is to give you something to think when you see things. You said when you saw rainbows, you thought,

'My heart leaps up when I behold a rainbow in the sky,' and you really thought rainbows deserved something better than that."

Lil loved in her the very things that had always irritated other people—her inappropriate, undeserved aristocratic air, her sentimentality, her irrationality, her belief that it's all right to say things hurt when they do, her tendency to quote poetry. It was overwhelming. Enough! Enough!

"But who held out her hand first?" Milly asked.

"I did."

"How did you dare?"

"By then I sort of knew you wouldn't chop it off. I figured the worst that could happen was you'd say no. But I knew you wouldn't run around telling everybody."

"That would have been worse than saying no?"

"Of course."

If there was a country where people didn't have to feel that way, Milly wanted to know when the next boat left. Sometimes she thought that God had given people everything they needed to be happy—touching, sleeping, eating, scratching itches, squeezing blackheads, shitting, pissing, farting, sneezing, sucking—and then people attached a taboo to each one, so you had to be a hero to get the good of it. Was that what Jesus meant when he said, "The kingdom of heaven is within *you*?"

"I didn't have to be very brave," Lil said, not impressed with being braver than Trude. "You were making calf eyes at me."

"I wasn't!"

"You got a pulse in your throat when you looked at me. You thought everything I said was wise or funny."

"It was, too."

"Everything happened very fast," Lil said.

"It took forever. I was kissing my pillow every night, asking it, 'Why are you making me wait so long?'"

"Three weeks isn't so long," Lil said.

Yes, there had been only three weeks between the snowy day Lil began to transform the big bleak shabby barracks of a house, and the night Milly found her waiting in the living room.

Milly had been putting the kids to bed, reading to them, kissing them goodnight, but they were already up again and jumping on the beds. The whole house creaked. From the stairs she saw Lil standing in the middle of the ugly gray rug. Lil had an unfamiliar look on her face, determined, a look of having, with difficulty, made up her mind. Was she going to say Milly's kids were too unruly? That she just couldn't take any more of such an undisciplined, unruly family? Milly was so scared. Maybe Lil was going to say she didn't like Milly's feeling for her. "I'm not one of *those*," Lil seemed to be going to say. That's how serious she looked.

"You kissed everybody but me," Lil said.

After all Milly's plans to be suave and masterful, she stood there like a kindergartener who has wet her pants. Lil laughed and stepped to her. Milly kissed her cheek, to stay strictly within the terms of the request, not to presume, but when she tried to step back Lil held her and made a row of kisses up her throat to her ear and caught the lobe and sucked it. Milly's knees came undone. She could have fallen. Against her ear, Lil whispered, "Can we sit down?" and the warm wind of the whisper went down Milly's neck and sides and leg and curled her toes.

"When I see your eyes I can't walk," Milly said. Lil covered her eyes and they made it to the chilly couch where they lay pressed utterly together in all their clothes, breathing, just breathing, like shipwrecked sailors cast up on the shore. Breathing was enough. They generated a little too much heat, but could not pull their bodies apart to take their clothes off.

The next day, it took everything Milly had to open

Sunup Motors but it seemed important, as a tribute to love, to do her duty. She spent the day radiating benevolence and remembering ("I was afraid I'd never be alive again," "You have such nice cheeks," "I always wanted to feel this way") feeling all the touches again fresh as the originals, pouring her whole soul forward to the evening.

Supper, kids, radio, bedlam, a cheery letter to Barney, then the distant rumble of beds being jumped on. It felt like silence at last. Lil was waiting beside the couch. She hadn't changed her mind. They fell together like hands. They breathed. Milly said, "All day I've wondered how I could have held you for ten hours without taking advantage of my opportunities. And I see I'm going to do the same thing again."

"It's nice to know we're really like this," Lil said. "I was afraid it couldn't be this way twice."

"We may have to try for comes."

"Have to?"

"To get it all in one place. It's everywhere now. There's no natural end to what we're doing."

But when she reached under the wartime winter layers of cloth—woollen slacks, long johns—and found Lil's generous, abundant, bountiful wet, her hand was awed. "Oh!" she said. "How beautiful!"

"Don't you know it's been this way for weeks, for you?"

"If one more beautiful thing happens, I'll have a heart attack and die," Milly said.

So staying still in each other's wet was added to breathing. Then stroking so light their skins had to reach up to it. Kisses soft or firm. There were no rules. They learned to survive more urgent touches. "I want to come for you. I want to give you that," Lil said, "but I don't know how." Her delicious shudders may or may not have been orgasms.

They never knew, and it didn't matter. Eventually they got to everything, even reading.

* * * * *

One night Lil took *Life on the Mississippi*, not unkindly, out of Milly's hands and snapped it shut. "Darling?" she said. Beware of questions that start with darling. "What have you told Barney about me?"

"Well, that you're here, of course. That things go much better now. The house runs smoothly." Then, to give the impression of really struggling for completeness, Milly said, "Mostly I tell him about the garage. That's what really interests him. Art Sweeney's car and so on." She began to develop the theme of Art Sweeney's car, but Lil was impossible to distract or divert when she had a topic in mind.

"Is that all?" Lil asked.

"No, he likes to hear about other people's cars, too."

"Come on, Mildred." Beware of someone who is calling you by your full name. Milly's parents had always been able to stop her in midair by calling her Mildred. Next Lil would start tapping her foot.

"I don't want to tell him about us in a letter," Milly said. "When he's safe home again is soon enough."

"So you're letting him think he has something great waiting for him, when he doesn't?"

"Well, not *great*. But, yeah, more of the same. Which might *seem* great compared with having kamikaze pilots crashing on you."

Lil didn't know about things like kamikaze pilots because she hated and avoided news and never read Milly's *Time* magazine. But there was no hope she'd ask for an explanation. What a terrible thing a one-track mind is.

Lil said, "Why don't you assume he's an adult? I think when you've had a big change in your life, you have a right to know it. He might have plans of his own."

"Right now he's in mortal danger," Milly said. A tenable position at last.

"He *has* had a big change in his life, hasn't he?" Lil asked.

Barney already knew all about Milly's Tendency. Who else might she have told? He took it surprisingly well, because he was sure he could fix her. He was very accepting, understanding, interested and curious, even though she had nothing to tell him about except fantasies. Since both the psychological literature and folk wisdom agreed that all any woman like her needed was a good fuck, Barney and Milly had high hopes for a while. She had no wish to spend her life needing what the world was conspiring to deny her. It seemed a little condescending to take such a fine man like a pill, but he was ever ready, an eager physician, an eager student of new positions and erogenous zones, and long after she concluded none of that was going to work he refused to give up. Of course he finally had to, but he kept forgetting.

She had to tell him many times, at least once a month, that his cure was not working. Especially when she was menstruating, she found it impossible to share a bed with him. He would get out of bed and come downstairs and find her at the kitchen table writing love letters she wouldn't dream of mailing, drinking, weeping, and he'd say, "What's the matter?" He seemed never to tire of hearing her answer.

The question would enrage her. "You *know* what's the matter," she'd snarl. "Why make me keep saying it?"

Not put off, he would say, "Tell me again," and when he had poked enough she would empty like an abscess, saying, "What's the matter is that I'm queer and I should never have got married and I should never have had kids and I'm living the wrong life and it's too late to start another, and that's what's the matter. So what do you know you didn't know before?"

He would take it in, about as perturbed as though she were reporting a headache or aphids on a rose, not very perturbed, hardly at all, and ask for details. He loved details. What did she want? She wanted to be held against a woman's body. She wanted the ache taken out of her heart. She wanted to be healed. She wanted a mother.

Once Barney said, "Your mother's nice. If you asked her to hug you, she'd do it. She wouldn't say, 'Back off, you monster,' or anything."

"Oh, no, not my *real* mother. I want a mother *substitute*," Milly said, and heard herself and laughed. Sometimes Barney really did help make things clear.

Another time he said, "If I wanted something that much, I'd go after it."

"You son of a bitch!" she cried. "When you're the reason I can't! You pull my wings off and then despise me for not flying."

But when her resentment settled down, in a day or two, she saw he had freed her, and she was grateful, though she would have preferred to be freed by her own efforts. If you need somebody else's permission to be free, you're probably really not. But why quibble? Free, she began her timid and awkward and barren courtship of Trude. Grateful, she got pregnant with Betty.

Her own fault, of course, but partly Barney's too. She was, briefly, imagining a big clear world where people didn't choke each other in the name of love. Was he imagining something as unlikely as that? But how could he forget, even in the heat of the moment, that she was an unfit mother? Did he deliberately keep setting her up to fail and fail? Couldn't he find something else to do with the pitiful suffering blunt instrument that she felt so guilty toward? Weren't men supposed to get sick of their wives?

Milly was so grouchy and depressed during that long boring pregnancy that everyone took it for granted she didn't very much like Betty, the cause of it all. They didn't understand, and Milly didn't tell them—Milly and Betty were veterans of the same siege, comrades forever. Milly adored Betty and found having a daughter a whole new experience—the incredible speed of her development, her vigor, her sturdy confidence, her indifference to reproach—not at all like the two tender, languid, madonna-like boys. Betty was a little thug.

I was never like that, Milly thought, not yet knowing she had been. Betty, she thought, isn't going to need some man's permission for *any*thing.

When Betty was seven months old and already walking, June came back into Milly's life. A friend telephoned and said, "I've got somebody here who went to the university with you."

"Bring her over," Milly said, and there was June, still the short-haired, breezy cowboy, windblown, but clumsily disguised in a pink dress, a marriage, and maybe fifty extra pounds. She had become a psychologist, which to Milly meant someone who knows and understands and forgives everything, someone to whom nothing human is alien. June had been up and down the earth since school, since the night she said, "You look sweet enough to kiss," and Milly said, "I like you so much—please tell me you're not queer," making June laugh and laugh but never offer another kiss, though within a day Milly was dying for one and hinting.

Barney, who knew all of Milly's stories, including that one, said, "Maybe she's the one," a possibility so breathtaking that Milly felt cautious about agreeing, lest the gods overhear and jinx everything. But she was, after all, older, wiser, in every way an improvement on her blundering sophomore self, so she risked whispering, "Maybe."

The next day Milly was lying under the apple tree in the back yard. Betty, wearing only a huge double-thickness wet diaper, was playing in the sandbox. June dropped by to borrow a book. Never before had Milly's library been of any practical benefit. June could drop by every day for hundreds of days. June sat down in the lopsided lawn chair Milly had built. Betty, sensing competition, mounted Milly's belly like a horse, soaking Milly's shirt with that dismaying diaper, bouncing up and down. You bet your life you've got competition, baby, Milly thought, looking up at June's slightly jowly, noble head, her black hair streaked with white against the pure sky. "You're beautiful," Milly said, wondering how many such declarations got made in urine-soaked sandy shirts.

June was serious and quiet for so long that Milly wished she'd chosen a time when her other attachments weren't jumping on her. She must have looked scared, because at last June said, "You don't trust anybody, do you?"

"Uh, well, that's a fault the world doesn't do much to help you get over," Milly said.

"I can't *tell* you, 'Trust me,' " June said. "You'll just have to find out for yourself that you can," and Milly instantly trusted her, root and branch, hammer and tongs, life and death, body and soul, blood sweat and tears.

"I'd like to play a little game with you," June said. "What do you think when I say *red?*"

What Milly thought was, Ah, my untrusting darling is considering a scary step, but what she said, quick as a wink, was "Rose." If June wanted a clean bill of mental health, Milly would provide it. She could play little games too. You'd never catch her thinking *blood* or *red-handed*. She didn't mind being tested. It even seemed like a good idea. She minded June's thinking she was too stupid to know what was happening. The unthinkable possibility was that June herself was stupid. ("I'd like to play a little game," for God's sake!)

"This is fun," Milly said. "Ask me another."

"*Mother*," June said.

"*Father*," Milly said.

And so on.

Apparently Milly passed, because when June was leaving she said, "Friend Husband will be going to a meeting Tuesday night. Want to keep me from getting lonesome?"

"I'd love to," Milly said maturely, concealing her crazy joy.

Friend Husband, whose name was Tom, hadn't left when Milly got there. He was a big rumpled Irishman, a lot older than June, white-haired. Milly set herself to charm him, and overdid it. His big laugh came barreling out at everything she said, and he wouldn't have gone to his meeting if June hadn't solemnly reminded him, "They're counting on you."

The house felt twice as roomy and airy without him, but still, frankly, small and hot. It was stacked with the collections of someone who couldn't throw anything away. June sat in a wooden rocking chair, as unapproachable as the moon. Milly sat on the couch, approachable.

"Everybody likes Tom," June said.

"Barney, too. Everybody likes Barney."

"And you? Do they like you?"

June was looking at her but Milly couldn't look back, not yet. "Uh, some do, I guess," she said.

June had a way of saying things that didn't quite follow, didn't quite fit on. This time it was, "You're a respectable matron."

It meant June had asked around. Good. If you get A on your word-association test and have a good reputation, that should take care of the preliminaries. Milly forced herself to look at June, to endure the dazzle of those clear gray eyes, but June looked away, saying, apparently to a potted plant, "Tell me something. When you disagree with the world, do you think the world's wrong or do you think you're wrong?"

If only the answer to that had been as obvious as red and rose. Thinking you're right and the whole world's wrong is the folk definition of insanity. But whose opinion might you hold except your own? Reluctantly, Milly said, "I think the world's wrong." Certain she had flunked, she hung her head and closed her eyes, contemplating the terrible months it would take to grow back her turtle shell, her barbed-wire heart. Then June's hand was under her chin, tilting her face up.

"It's time you had somebody on your side," June said, and placed on Milly's mouth the kiss that confirmed a lifetime's guesses. Yes, it was what Milly had thought it would be. Yes, she had looked for the right remedy, as a sick animal knows which plant to eat. June's kiss was the specific for Milly's complaint. Safe in June's firm warm hug, Milly whispered, "I love you. I loved you the first time I saw you."

June said, "Careful. Tom will be getting home soon."

"Umm. Maybe he'll stop somewhere along the way."

"Not him. So don't get worked up."

"I'm very calm."

"I don't believe you."

Still not believing each other, they met on Tuesdays during Tom's meeting, the only time all week he was away. How could an experienced lesbian like June, how could someone as passionate as Milly, be satisfied with schoolgirl kisses? They should have believed each other and stayed with the kisses. Schoolgirls should be that lucky.

Milly was so happy she was even able to keep Barney satisfied. It wouldn't have been fair to put him through all the bad times and then not let him share the good. Anyway, he was her dear friend and she loved him. She wanted to reward his understanding and generosity, but mostly keep his jealous demon from waking up and making trouble. To her relief, he was simply pleased. He kept her busy.

Then one Tuesday June greeted Milly in a wildly brilliant kimono with slits under the sleeves through which Milly could see for the first time June's breasts, low, smallish, downward-tending. Milly started to reach inside, but June caught her hand, held her still, and undressed her. Then they lay down face to face.

"So serious," June said.

"I don't take this lightly. And I don't think you do, either."

"Close eyes," June said, and though Milly longed to see, she obeyed. June put her hand between Milly's legs and held, simply held, her there, and with the other, or rather with one fingertip of the other, she drew a fine, light, sparkling, silver line down Milly's side from armpit to hip, and then again and then again and then again, and the little waves all over Milly's body became big ones that didn't stop until she was too tired for more. She had never used some of those muscles before. Even her ribs ached. She was so wet she was afraid June would think she had a disease, but June seemed to know all about that.

Milly was smiling and kissing, overwhelmed with happiness and gratitude, saying, "You got it all out for me, for the first time in my life it's all out," when June suddenly said, "Can I ask you something?"

"*Any*thing," Milly said.

"Why couldn't Barney do that?" Barney? Who's he?

"Because I'm a lesbian," Milly said proudly.

"Nonsense. You're no more a lesbian than I am."

Milly shouldn't have laughed. Laughing was a mistake, brought on by being so relaxed and happy, ready to laugh at anything. And using that word was a mistake, brought on by forgetting that people are willing to do a lot of things they're not willing to call by their correct names.

Getting dressed, June said, "By the way, when you teach Barney to do that, best you shouldn't say where you learned it." (Then Milly knew the right answer was, "He doesn't know how.")

"I don't want it from anyone but you," Milly said across the wall June was building between them. "Darling, it's not what somebody does, it's what it *means*. It's in our minds. You know that."

"In fact, it's simple stimulus-response," June said, aloof, far away.

"It's not. It is not. You're pretending I would have felt all that if an old shoe had touched me, or my grandpa."

"Just don't tell Barney where you learned it."

End of discussion. End forever, it turned out, though June came to Milly's house almost every afternoon to play with Betty or weed the flowerbeds, while Milly sulked and glowered, thinking extreme metaphors like "You laid your egg in my heart and the larva hatched and is eating me" or "You tied my gut to your saddle and are dragging me across a desert." June said, "I do believe you're jealous of your own child." Sundays June brought Tom, and Milly would have to pull herself together and amuse him. He was delighted by all her struggling little witticisms, her cute way of saying things. June said, "I do believe you like to be the center of attention." After they left, Milly would howl at the ceiling.

She delayed working on her turtle shell, her barbed wire, because she was waiting for June's emotion to get out of hand again. Perhaps it did that at a certain point in June's menstrual cycle. No. Well, perhaps it was seasonal; wait a year. At the end of a year, she asked June not to come again.

Milly never knew how strong she was until she didn't die over June. It was a close call. Being alone would have helped. She longed to be alone and very quiet, to turn her soul into a tiny hard seed that could hold out for better weather, but as her power to live decreased her family's demands rushed into the vacuum. Barney was especially difficult. The children seemed to understand, sometimes, a little, about ebbing and flowing, and in any case they were certain she loved them. They needed simple, practical things, like food, hugs, praise, and clean clothes, that were usually more or less possible. But Barney needed the soul that was longing to hibernate. He needed understanding, companionship, conversation, beauty, union, sex—especially sex. Of course, but why from her?

He took to coming home at odd hours during the day. When you're your own boss you can do that. He seemed to think he was being extra helpful during this hard time she was having, really standing by, really a rock for her. He was showing his undiminished love despite her peculiarities. He was providing, at all hours and wherever she might try to hide, his sturdy shoulder, his endless sympathy. Even when she climbed out the window and hid on the roof he found her. Solitude had never been his idea of a good time, and he was sparing her the torment of being alone, those terrifying empty hours.

She had to wonder what her own illusions were and whether they stuck out like Barney's.

Like a big kindly daddy—refuge and protector—he would enfold her. In half a minute his prick would be prodding her. You could set your watch by it, but he was always surprised; his intention was so entirely other. The first few times she felt so sorry for him that she gave in. After all, he suffered over her as she suffered over June. Freed of his garbage, he would hop up refreshed and go back to work, while she paced the floor. She couldn't stand still to take a shower. She couldn't stop crying. She had to learn to say no. He had to learn to bear his deprivations. They had to have a talk.

He said he was worried about her, and part of the reason he came home so much was that he was afraid she might kill herself, much as he hated to mention such a possibility, or that she might harm the kids. She knew how much she was drinking, didn't she?

She said she regarded drinking as a temporary, reversible suicide and she'd deal with it later on when she felt better. If he was so worried about her, why did he feel peppy and cheerful after he made her crazy? She said sex drove her crazy right then, and she supposed she was jealous, as a heart might be if it had to pump blood to every other organ but got none for itself. The Bible, harsh as it was, forbade the muzzling of the ox that threshes the grain. If even the mean old Bible knew that about humble oxen, what might kind Barney know about Milly? In short, she could no longer give what she did not get. She didn't see how other women did it.

He said he really did intend to be nice and the sex was an accident, a reflex. At one time he had supposed it would comfort her as it did him, but he'd learned better—and why didn't it?

She said she thought homosexuality was probably a natural part of everybody, because everybody has a deprivation to make up or a pleasure to repeat, and suppressing homosexuality made people sick. Maybe suppressing it even caused war.

He said she was sicker since she stopped suppressing it than she was before.

She said she was not sick but merely suffering. She had used up the peace and energy she had brought from her mother's body, and until she got a new supply Barney would have to wait. She had used up her principal, to put it in terms a Sunup would understand.

He said he had not deserved that, because, for the son of a former tycoon, he thought remarkably rarely about principal.

She said he was right and she was sorry. She said men should love men and women should love women and then maybe they'd be able to love each other. First things first.

He said he, personally, didn't think he could get worked up about a flat hairy chest.

She said he offered one to her as an object of desire, so didn't that mean he thought it was pretty exciting? Otherwise, why did he expect her to? How might something that repelled him attract her?

He said women are supposed to be opposite to and complementary to men.

She said they belonged to the same species and she was like him in every way, in detail. She needed and wanted exactly what he needed and wanted.

He said he was eager for her to have what she needed and get their life and their home back on course. He would have been very glad if things had worked out with June, except that he would have preferred an unmarried woman who could live in their house.

What?

"Well, to me that would be ideal," he said.

"I am stunned."

"While you're stunned, here's another. I've been thinking of going to New York or Chicago or San Francisco, some place like that, and bringing back a lesbian for you."

Milly kept shaking her head and making little random amazed noises. Barney looked pleased, as though immune to being boring and predictable from then on.

He said, "You must have known I'd do *some*thing. You know I'm a man of action." It was one of his favorite beliefs about himself.

"How did you think you'd catch one? With a butterfly net?"

"I'd ask a cab driver where their bars are. Then I'd spread the word in the bars and wait for somebody to get in touch with me. I figured somebody down on her luck might be interested."

(Here comes Barney wheeling into the driveway. Beside him is a strange, defeated creature, a true unfortunate, an anomalous castoff down on its luck. In its eyes, Milly can read a promise of love.)

"You'd really put up with that?" Milly asked.

"I figured it could go two ways."

"At least two."

"One, you'd realize that wasn't what you wanted after all, so you'd settle down and make the most of what you have." He was the finest of men, but did he *have* to use his fingers to count to two? "Two, you'd be satisfied and then we could all be happy."

"And you'd go along with that?"

"Yes, I would," Barney said solemnly. "I know there would be problems, but yes I would."

But would Lil go along with it? Milly wasn't ready to ask her. There was something tough and realistic in Lil, practical, unsentimental. She could love, gloriously, without stint, but you couldn't exactly call her a fool for love. You could doubt that Lil would sacrifice everything in order to spare Milly from having to sacrifice anything. Milly wanted more time to become irreplaceable, essential, before she risked a proposal that was actually ideal, for her as well as for Barney, but might seem to Lil grubby, cowardly, corrupt, unthinkable.

Lil said again, "Barney has had a big change in his life, hasn't he?"

"Has he?" Milly squeaked.

"You know it," Lil said.

"Then I guess I'd better tell him," Milly said.

She was going to leave it at that, intended to, but un-expectedly said, "Actually, I've mentioned it to him already."

"You make me feel like a fool," Lil said. "Pretend I'm and adult and tell me the things that are my business, okay?"

"I wanted to. But, darling, it's complicated."

"And getting more."

"He's pleased. He wants you to stay on here after he gets home. He thinks you're just what the family needed. He wants me to be happy."

"Oh, brother!"

"I didn't know how you'd feel about that," Milly said.

"I feel like pacing the floor, that's how I feel," Lil said, jumping up and pacing rapidly to the wall, whirling around and starting over. "I feel like yelling, 'How *could* you?'"

"We can talk about it later," Milly said, really intimi-dated.

"When I've come to my senses?"

"I'm sorry I brought it up."

"You didn't bring it up. I did."

"I'm sorry you did."

"You wanted everything to just sort of *happen*. I'd be the maid-of-all-work, and you'd be sneaking from his bed to mine, and sometimes he'd want to come along, and it would be too mean to say no when he's being so understanding, and maybe he'd want to just watch, and maybe he'd want to play too, and it wouldn't be anybody's fault because it just *happened*. How could you? God damn it, how could you even consider doing such a thing to our love?"

Milly said, "It wouldn't be that way," shocked at Lil's dirty mind but not wanting to say so and make Lil madder.

While Milly was waiting to think of something peace-making to say a very unwelcome memory intruded:

Milly: I was afraid you'd divorce me or have me de-clared insane or something. But you really don't seem to mind. I think you like me queer.
Barney: Well, at the back of a guy's mind there's always the thought, like, I can show her what's really good.
Milly: I don't think that's it. I think women making love together is just a damn aphrodisiac idea, that's all.
Barney, reluctantly: Yeah.

It was a memory that cut the ground out from under moral indignation, but Milly did her best. "You're letting your imagination run wild," she said. "Barney and I—"

"The way you say that! 'Barney and I!' You're really married. After everything, you're really married!"

"Barney and I," Milly repeated sturdily, "have been try-ing to work out a way to hold the marriage together for the sake of the kids. This seemed like one way to do it, that's all. He wouldn't bother us. He'd be a father for Jack. You'd have a home. What if you did seem to be the maid-of-all-work? *We'd* know you are my mate and darling and savior and holy angel and heart's blood and every blessing. We need to keep up appearances. You don't know how cruel the world is. If you think it's going to rise up and call us beautiful, just because we are, you're a nut."

Lil, somewhat mollified despite herself, stopped pacing and cuddled against Milly's side on the couch. "Look who's calling who a nut," she said fondly. "Some nuts think they can be thrashing around tearing up the sheets and horny husbands will fall alseep down the hall. No and no and no and no and no."

"At least think about it," Milly said.

"And no. I mean, yes, of course I will. I can even make myself believe a cat won't lick the butter, but don't hold your breath."

* * * * *

A certain bomb went off in Japan, and then another. It seemed like a good idea at the time. The point right then was that the bleeding was stopped sooner than expected, and whoever wasn't dead of it could live to die some other way, maybe even of old age.

The news brought a unanimous nationwide exhalation, so vast the moon must have felt the wind of it. Then Milly and Lil and the kids drove downtown to be part of whatever else the great collective heart of the nation was doing. They got caught in a honking traffic jam, honked their own horn a lot, listened to the radio bringing sounds of bedlam from Times Square, whooped out the car windows at other whoopers, disentangled themselves, and went home. There should have been something else to do, some solemn, majestic way to express relief and gratitude. Some music grand beyond imagination. Some noble words. The human spirit, Milly concluded, is magnificent except when good things happen.

She thanked God, whatever that might be, for saving Barney, for not granting the horrible little wish she did not always succeed in being unaware of. Yes, Circumambient Something, I have envied Lil her lack of conflict. Yes, I have wished my choices could be as uncomplicated as hers. But I'm very glad to leave omnipotence to you and have Barney alive to be dealt with in the regular human way.

Lil began to read the newspaper, not, as Milly first hoped, because the news was now less ghastly, but because she was planning to leave. She was reading the want ads, looking for a job and an apartment.

Milly said, "Barney's hitch is for duration plus one year. There's no hurry." Then the Navy announced how many points were needed for discharge. She added up Barney's. Seventeen points for being thirty-four years old, eighteen for thirty-six months' service, seven for twenty-eight months overseas, ten for having dependents. Fifty-two, more than enough. He could have been home yesterday. She began to expect him to appear unannounced, perhaps to be dropped from a plane into the backyard. She could picture the parachute tangled in the apple tree, and Barney, all smiles, waving and yelling. She had to be glad. She could not have tolerated herself if she hadn't been glad. But the simple time with Lil was over. From now on, it would be complicated.

Their bodies felt the hurry, felt in every touch the danger of goodbye, and the hot, wild, obsessive stage came again. They had been so comfortable, so domestic and calm. Passion, Milly realized with the part of her mind that was not engulfed, is to melt people together. Once they're together, it's not necessary.

When they weren't making love, they were arguing.

"Do you know what I'd have to do to get a divorce? I'd have to accuse Barney of all kinds of shitty things he hasn't done, and I'd have to get witnesses who would swear they saw him do them. Or I'd have to pay a detective to break in and take a picture of him committing adultery."

"Go to Reno."

"I can't go to Reno."

"You don't need a divorce anyway. Just leave him."

"He needs a wife. He needs to be free to find one."

"Just leave him and let him divorce you. He can hire a detective to take our picture."

"You'd like that, wouldn't you?"

"*Yes!* I want everybody to see how much you love me. I'm proud of how much you love me."

That would start them up again, nothing fancy, just

134

locked together full length gasping and sweating. Lil's thigh between Milly's legs and all it took, something to brace against, something to resist—that and Lil's gingersnap eyes, which Milly pretended not to notice, watching all proud, serene, and powerful.

"I wish Barney could see how I can excite you and he can't."

"Aha, you *would* like to live here and let him watch!"

"Nope."

"Admit it."

"Nope."

Lil admitted nothing that did not suit her purposes. She was entirely ruthless. She didn't have a fair bone in her body. It was even possible sometimes to prefer Barney—the long, candid conversations, the adjustments and compromises, cards on the table, man to man. You could *deal* with somebody like Barney. You could *get* somewhere. Lil's idea of bargaining was to go for your throat.

This ostentatious want-ad reading, for instance. She had private time aplenty to do that, but she chose to let Milly find her doing it, knowing Milly would be driven clean out of her mind.

Maybe Lil was, in her own demonic way, acknowledging that you had to be crazy to do what she wanted. You're not crazy enough to destroy your home, to tear your children from their father? We'll fix that in a jiffy. "Do you think I'd like peddling cosmetics door to door? Do you think I could find a nice woman to take care of Jack a few hours a day?"

Lil broke her ankle, too. The woman would stop at nothing. That fine, bright, springy, glossy mare of a body decided to collapse in a heap on its elegant ankle, as though to say "I won't stand for this." Much time was spent elevating the pitiful white cast, working crossword puzzles, crocheting. There was a little heartbreaking hobbling on a too-short crutch. The house reverted to its former grubbiness. Milly had to cook after a hard day at the garage. Dirty clothes piled up. The doctor said Lil would be good as new in about six weeks. Don't *do* this to me, Lil. I *always* appreciated you. I do not need to be taught how much I need you.

But, false as Lil herself, all Milly said was, "Can I get you anything, darling?"

* * * * *

Milly spoke to Earl as rarely as possible, nothing beyond the minimum amenities a Sunup could not omit, such as "good morning," and the impersonal shorthand of running the garage. He was, in fact, an excellent salesman. His peculiar combination of boredom and contempt kept him silent while the customers argued out both sides alone; they ended up wanting to prove to him they could easily afford the car. Earl had a reflex that woke him up at the exactly correct moment for whipping out his book and writing up the sale. If Earl hadn't had certain problems, he would have had plenty of money and it wouldn't have been up to Barney to make sure nobody named Sunup went to school shabby.

When Milly heard herself telling Earl, "My housekeeper is on strike," she was as surprised as he was. She realized that she had no close friends. She had been afraid to have friends because it hurt so much when she fell in love with them, and by the time Lil ended that danger, Milly was habituated to keeping her problems inside. See what you've driven me to, Lil—I'm talking to *Earl,* I'm feeling a reluctant sympathy with him. He's lost his woman's care. He's getting scruffy. He doesn't know what to do.

"Gertrude's on strike, too," Earl said. He sounded almost plain and simple. That is, he did not say, "My so-called helpmate is also indulging in a work-stoppage."

"I noticed the scorch on your cuff," Milly said.

"I had to iron it myself." His voice was an indignant whine, but Milly understood. "Gertrude doesn't do anything any more. I thought she'd come to her senses when the war was over and Spragg's laid her off. But no."

"She's been laid off?"

"They're calling it that. Actually, by the time they retool, the men will be home, wanting their jobs back. And the women, praise the Lord, will stay home and be women again—if they remember how. If they ever knew."

Inasmuch as Earl should be the last person to question anyone's claim to maleness or femaleness, he was no doubt merely blundering, merely being his usual damn fool self, uncritically blathering standard opinions. Milly decided not to have a delusion of reference. It would lead to retaliation, which was mean, or to trying to prove she was a real woman. All the troubles of her life had come from trying to prove she was a real woman.

"I was thinking I might ask Ione or Ruby to help me out until Lil's better. But maybe I'll ask Trude."

"Ask them all. You're welcome to the lot. They're all entirely worthless. Gertrude has taught our daughters none of the so-called womanly arts. They try, but they're just underfoot. They get in my way when I iron."

"I was hoping for some cooking. Laundry. Maybe a little, uh, ironing. Somebody to sweep up sometimes. Change the sheets."

"For you, Gertrude might do it. For me, she does nothing." His voice broke, bewildered. He was up against absolute mystery, inscrutability, injustice, malice—after all he'd done for Trude.

* * * * *

Once again the house smelled of good things in the oven when Milly got home. The clothes were clean again. The dust balls were gone. God knew where Trude found the time. As far as Milly could tell, all Trude did was yatter with Lil. Lil would be lying on the couch with her cast resting on the couch back, no doubt in pain, laughing her head off, making Milly remember how long it had been since she herself had made Lil laugh. Trude, young and cute these days, would be telling stories—about the Zyglo Line, about Earl, about her childhood—not really all that funny, but full of descriptions and details. Lil's laughter acknowledged experiences she recognized, not wit. Trude's simple, natural interst in the world reminded Milly how narrow and inward-turned she herself was, how unlikely to notice anything that didn't bear on her own obsessions.

The kids, who had been engrossed in their own lives, uninterested in their home except as a convenience, now could hardly be torn from it. They too loved their Aunt Trude's stories and sat solemnly at her feet like disciples. Why weren't they out playing kickball in this perfect autumn weather, like normal children? Milly hoped Trude wasn't giving them bad habits. The last thing Milly wanted was their full attention.

After supper, she would take Trude home. That is, Trude drove and Milly went along to bring the car back. Alone with her like that, listening to her chatter, Milly would remember that she really did love Trude and that it was nice to see her chatty and sassy. Milly just had to learn to love her differently, enjoying her instead of pitying and protecting her and getting indignant in her behalf. A Trude who didn't scurry around in an anxious little trot could also be loved.

"Your job really changed you," Milly said one evening.

"Yes," Trude said proudly.

"You must be sorry to see it end."

"Oh, I'll do something else. I won't go back to like I was. I found out it's not some huge scary thing just men can do, to make money. I used to think men went out and took money away from lions or something. Me and my friend Ada, we're talking about starting a restaurant, I mean a hamburger stand. Greasy spoon, Ada calls it. She's so funny. I'll get by. Barney doesn't have to risk his neck so I can make money."

"Barney's due home now."

"Thank the Lord!"

"And I don't want to go back either."

"Oh, it will be so wonderful to have him home."

"Well, I'm glad too, of course, but I don't want to go back. I've had some changes too."

"But you *always* had money."

"It's not money."

"For me, it's money."

"It was having friends that changed you. Talking to people. Getting out of the house. Seeing the world, so to speak."

"No, it was money. Of my own. My friend Crystal, she did all like that, but she didn't change. Because she didn't get to keep her money. I got you to thank."

"Me?"

"I used you to scare Earl to not take my money. Did you know Earl's scared of you? I know you like Earl, but you scare him."

Milly decided not to answer; women don't like to have anyone but themselves criticize their husbands, even the worst husbands. But how could anybody imagine that she liked Earl?

Trude said, still chattily, "I always know when he's done, you know, *it*, because he always washes and washes and washes the next day. He's so funny."

Milly felt her whole body blush. That she had been so stupid. That Trude knew. That Earl had felt dirty the next day. Milly stayed still and silent and felt the blushes surging and surging. If she'd been driving, she'd have had a wreck.

Trude was driving very competently, not upset at all. "He'll do it to anybody but me," she said. "But that's okay. I don't want him now. I can't remember why I ever did. I used to be crying for it. I used to tell myself he just wasn't very sexy. But I always knew. I'm thinking I might divorce him."

"There's no advantage to you in that," Milly choked, picturing herself as co-respondent, picturing huge banner headlines, newsboys crying, "Extra, Extra, Read All About It."

"It would just make me feel better," Trude said. "It would just tell Earl enough is enough."

"But the Sunups don't divorce. No Sunup has ever been divorced."

"I'm not a Sunup. I'm an Emerson. I just found out that's a pretty good name too. Did you ever hear of Ralph Walter Emerson?"

"I doubt the Emersons divorce either."

"This Emerson just might. He killed my babies. All those poor babies turned blue because he made me cry all the time."

"I've been meaning to tell you. They've found the cause of blue babies. There's something called the Rh factor. When the mother doesn't have it and the baby inherits it from the father, the mother's body thinks the baby's a foreign body and tries to kill it. The baby gets erythroblastosis foetalis, because the mother has something like an allergy to it." Milly didn't know how much of that got through. Trude, true to Milly's training, did not take her eyes off the road.

At last Trude said, "You're saying it was my fault."

"I'm saying it was nobody's fault."

"It was Earl's fault, because he's no damn good."

* * * * *

There was a marching band at the station to meet Barney: Rusty on kazoo, Murray on comb, Betty on tambourine, Jack on oatmeal box, Milly and Trude with a Welcome Home banner and loud rum-tum-tums. When the train came into sight, the band struck up *Anchors Aweigh*, fairly passably, and stayed with it until four old ladies, a dog, and a tall handsome commander in gold-encrusted black with about thirty square inches of battle ribbons near his left lapel came down the iron steps to the platform. Then the commander disappeared entirely under hugging bodies and only the oatmeal box played on.

The band was subject to fits. It regrouped and escorted the commander up the sidewalk to his house, this time with *Stars and Stripes Forever.* The maples and oaks found a hundred ways to say red. The sky said one clear blue.

I'm really glad, Milly thought, relieved. I'm really glad to see him.

But what's a wedding without a specter? In the front hall, bravely aslant on her crutch, stood Lil. "Hello, Commander."

"Your crutch is too short. I'll fix it. Call me Barney," he said, and hugged her.

He had to go to the bathroom right away. As always, coming home gave his bowels a good idea. How had he managed for three years? Trude and the kids followed him upstairs and hovered outside the bathroom door.

Lil used that short privacy to whisper, "I've got to get out of here. I can't handle this."

Milly saw that Lil was having an attack of Only a Woman, and there was no time to persuade her out of it.

"You didn't tell me he was handsome. You didn't tell me he was *nice*," Lil hissed. "I was expecting a sleazy used-car dealer. There's no scrambled egg on *my* cap."

"Stop it, please."

"I'm supposed to say, to *that*, 'Tough luck, fella, I'm taking your wife and kids away?' "

"Stop it."

" 'Hey, fella, back off or I'll slug you—on the shin!' "

"Darling, I beg you—"

"I'm supposed to sleep here tonight and listen to your yips and yowls? Forget it!"

"Darling—"

"I'll be gone. I swear I'll be gone."

"Darling, it's *you* that made me want to not die."

"I'll be at my folks' house for a while. After that, I don't know where."

"You're being so damn unfair," Milly said, and then came the roar of rushing water. Before the whole troop was downstairs again, she managed to squeeze in, "What in hell do you want me to do?"

"I'd like you to take Jack and me to my folks' house. Could you do that?" Lil asked, sociably.

Barney said, "First let me lengthen that crutch." He loosened the wing-nut, pulled out the extender, tightened the nut again. Milly was embarrassed. Why hadn't she done that? "Do you really have to go?" he asked. "I'm taking everybody out to dinner."

"Yes, I really have to," Lil said.

Trude said, "But, Barney, I'm getting dinner. I'm fixing everything you like best. Potato salad, and baked beans, and sliced tomatoes with dill and vinegar, and pork chops, and cherry pie—"

Jack said, "I don't want to go to Gramma's."

Barney said, "Are you putting eggs and radishes and pickles and onions in the potato salad?"

"Sure. Doesn't everybody?"

"There are parts of the world where they mix potatoes and mayonnaise and call it potato salad."

Trude laughed. "You're some kidder, Barney."

Jack said, "I don't want to go to Gramma's."

Lil picked up the suitcase she must have packed ahead of time. "Okay, Milly," she said.

In the car, Jack stiffened and wailed, something Milly would have liked to do too. "I want potato salad," he howled. "I want to stay with Barney. He smells good. He's nice. I don't like Gramma. I don't like Grampa."

"Do they even know you're coming?" Milly asked.

"I said I probably would."

"Oh, come on back!"

"Sleep with me tonight?"

"God, I hate these power plays. You know I can't. It's Barney's first night home.

"And he's so horny, and you're so glad to see him. I'm warning you, I'm not here to patch you up so you can be a better wife. If you take the goodness I put into your soul and give it to him, I'm not here at all."

"I have to spend time with him. I have to welcome him home. I have to talk with him."

"Uh huh."

"I really mean *talk*."

"Uh huh."

"So let's go home."

"No."

* * * * *

Milly really did mean talk, and even after his cock faithfully rose she kept on talking. Barney was groaning that he had missed her, that it was so unbelievably *good* to be home, and there was no way not to be touched by that, but she was afraid she would die if she lost Lil. Right then she did not even love Lil. She only knew she would die without her.

"Barney, would you mind awfully?"

"Headache? Hard day?" he asked bitterly.

"You know I never pulled that crap on you. It's Lil."

"Lil is not a problem. Lil is welcome."

"She's afraid. You're too impressive. You can't think how you look in that damn uniform. Formidable."

"I just wore it for the kids."

"Well, she's feeling outranked. And she's running away. And I'm scared. And I'm sorry. You did have a little fun while you were gone, I hope."

"Sure, but that's different. I love *you*." He got up and put on some pajamas as a chastity belt, a bundling board. Then he hurried back to the warm bed.

"So you're not exactly sex-starved," she said.

"What can I tell you? It was mechanical and mean and ugly. If I can't have something humane and caring, with some soul in it, I'd rather jerk off. I'm *love*-starved."

"Love I can give you," she said, and they smiled and held each other. It was a cold October night, perfect for hugging.

"I kind of wish," he said, "I'd followed up with Trude."

"Trude?"

"Yeah, Trude."

Milly's surprise was entirely fraudulent; she had a fully worked-out fantasy of Barney's marrying Trude and the happy ending that would provide for all parties. But surprise seemed wise until Barney arrived at the same fantasy in his own way, which was slow, stubborn, and resistant to suggestion.

"*Trude?*" she asked again.

"You could learn a lot from Trude," he said defensively. *Protectively.* Ah.

"I'm sure I could," Milly said, and because that sounded a little too warm and generous she added, "I like to think I can learn from anybody."

"At least she can live a woman's life without going crazy."

"Well, yes," grudgingly. ' "Actually, that's always impressed me, too. For a while I thought maybe I could catch it from her, like a disease." This to remind him that Milly had wanted Trude and been ignored. Surely he would like to outshine, outattract, outcourt, outperform somebody, and maybe Milly would do—even though she was only a woman.

Unfortunately, he had an alternate fantasy stuck in his stubborn head: Milly and Lil playing prettily, creating a surplus for him.

He said, "When I told you it was okay with me, I didn't expect you to leave me out."

"I never meant to. But Lil suspects you."

"Of what?"

"Oh, of, uh, having something more in mind. A triple bed or something."

"That's absurd."

"That's what I told her."

"She sure takes a lot on herself—for a housekeeper." (Milly had hoped he wouldn't say that.) "Who in hell does she think she is?"

It seemed best not to add to the dangers of the situation by telling him who Lil was.

He said, "She comes in here and takes over my house and takes over my wife and tells my wife not to sleep with me and who in hell is she? The housekeeper. She answered a want-ad."

"Well, it's complicated," Milly said carefully.

"All over this country tonight the men from my ship are getting a warm welcome home. I'm sure glad they can't see me now."

"You're being wonderful," Milly said, hoping he'd realize you can't rape somebody into a warm welcome home. "I really appreciate it."

"If you knew how I've thought about you."

"I know."

"I've been, hammy as it sounds, fighting for you. You wouldn't have liked what the Japs would have done to you. They are not nice people. You wouldn't have liked what the Krauts would have done, either."

"I know."

"So I get home from fighting for you, and you say, 'Sorry, the housekeeper told me not to,' and I say, 'Oh, all right. I understand. Sorry I was a pest.' A real man would bust right past this shit."

"Come on, you know you're a real man."

"I'm too damn nice. Did you know that the whole world despises this country for what we let women get away with?" (Who was this "we" that was letting half of itself get away with something?) "I should have put my foot down a long time ago. I should have taken what I needed and let you like me or not. You don't have to like me."

"If you hadn't been nice, we wouldn't have lasted a minute."

"In Japan, we would have lasted and you would have put out and shut up and you would have knelt when I came into the room."

"How you gonna keep 'em down on the farm, after they've seen Toke-Yo?" Milly sang, but he would not smile.

"Do you know why a tiny country like Japan attacked a huge country like America?" he asked. "They thought we couldn't fight. They thought we were pushovers. They thought we were sissies."

"Barney, America is a real country. You're a real man. The only question is, am I a real woman? If anybody's ever seen one of those."

"Trude's a real woman," Barney said, and smiled.

Milly saw he had resigned himself one more time to the degradation of being a good person.

* * * * *

Being too nice was not something Lil would ever have to worry about, Milly thought, driving to see her the next day. Just because her touch had freed Milly from despair, drinking, weeping, and three-week menstrual depressions, was that any reason for Lil to be so high-handed, rigid, unreasonable, demanding, possessive, one-way? There must have been something Milly's countertouch did for Lil, too, but did Milly press her advantage or become high-handed rigid, et cetera?

To Milly's surprise, Lil came out and climbed into the car. Milly had expected to be denied the chance to talk as well as the chance to kiss. She had expected to sit in the living room with Lil's parents, who would have considered it rude to leave the room.

"Boy, they're driving me nuts," Lil said. "My dad's got the ballgame on the radio. I'd like to tear it out by the roots. It shakes the house."

"Hi, Angel," Milly said.

"Jack's in hog heaven. They wait on him hand and foot. He sits in the living room and yells for my mother to bring him a glass of water. And she does it. Talk about your princes!"

Why give Lil a chance to say no? Without consulting her, Milly drove home. The kids were in school. Barney was at the garage. Milly went inside and waited while Lil and her cast and her crutch toiled up the path and clumped across the porch. They met with a groan on the formerly ugly formerly gray rug.

"Hi yourself," Lil said.

Afterward Lil wanted to know what Milly and Barney had done the night before, and was not entirely pleased to hear they had shared a bed, even though unsexually, just friends, just talking.

"Didn't you tell me you couldn't breathe in bed with

him?" Lil demanded. "Didn't you used to sleep in the guest room because he took all your air?"

Milly would not have let anyone else question her, and barely could let Lil. Was someone's having saved your life reason enough to let her question you?

"Last night was different. He'd been away so long. I didn't want to be mean."

"Well, at least I wasn't in the next room sweating it out," Lil said bitterly.

And finally Milly could see, yes, that would have been difficult for Lil, and not just for Lil. Difficult all around, in fact. And, reluctantly, Milly had to consider the possibility that Lil was not being unreasonable, was, perhaps, even working, in her sturdy wrongheaded little way, to prevent an irretrievable error, to prevent everybody's tone from being always bitter.

"Yes, it would have been terrible to have you in the next room," Milly said. "Why didn't I see that before? Why didn't you tell me?"

"I did."

"Why didn't you tell me *again?*"

"I did. A lot."

"Why didn't you tell me until I heard you?"

"I never thought you were dumb."

"Well, Barney's going to marry Trude, but it will take a while."

"Why can't we just go? You're not responsible to get him settled. You don't have to run his life. Maybe he'd like to pick out his own wife. How you do mother-hen him!"

"I want to leave in good order, after everybody is provided for. I don't want to drive him crazy."

"He seems sane enough. Give him that much credit. He's as sane as anybody else, anyway."

"Don't you see? I'm afraid he'll kill us." There it

was said. Lil took it in. It wouldn't have to be repeated.

"My God. You really think that could happen?"

"You bet I do. You bet I do."

"Wow. Well, if you say so. But what do I do in the meantime? I've got no place to live."

"Let's find you a little house near by."

"I've got almost no money."

"A cheap little place. You'll make it beautiful. You have a talent."

"I might have to leave town."

"Stop threatening me. I'm working as fast as I can."

"When I tell you something, you say I'm threatening you, and then you say I didn't tell you. I'm telling you, if I can't find a job here I might have to leave town."

"Let's find you a little house and you can work for me."

Lil thought a while and then said cautiously, "With that and my pension I might get by. I can't do much anyway till Jack's in school, and that's next fall. If I had to hire somebody to watch him, it'd cost all I could make. I sure don't want my mother to. So—okay." Lil gulped and said again, "Okay."

"Okay!" Milly said joyfully.

"Uh, honey?"

"What, love?"

"Sleep in the guest room?"

"Oh, God, here we go again!"

"Like you always did, before?"

"Why do you keep setting up these damned conditions?"

"But you will sleep in the guest room?"

"I guess so."

"I might make you feel so good you'd think you could take care of everybody, like you did when June was with you."

Did June leave because Milly slept with Barney? Was it as simple as that?

"Yes, I'll sleep in the guest room," Milly said.

* * * * *

While Lil's ankle finished healing, Trude maintained Milly's house and Milly spent her days as she preferred, fixing a sweet little four-room wreck, an unrecognized jewel that even the owner despised. Some men who worked at Spragg's had batched it there, unlovingly, and moved on when the war ended. It was a mess. But it had a bay window on the side and a porch with an arched roof on the front, and Milly knew a love nest when she saw one. She was very good at seeing and fixing, terrible at maintaining. She had a good time patching and painting, puttying in new window-panes, hauling trash to the dump, working fast to beat winter. When the landlady saw the possibilities, she had the outside painted. It looked great.

Nothing is perfect. There was no furnace, but a fairly decent coal-burning Kalamazoo heater. There was no hot water, but what did that matter?—there was no bathtub. Lil said she and Jack would bathe at Milly's, on the job. The kitchen had a chipped iron sink in the corner and a kerosene cookstove. No counters, no cupboards. "It's all right," Lil said. "I grew up with a kitchen like this. And it's just for a while. Remember, it's just for a while."

Barney hauled over some furniture and rugs. Lil hung curtains. The house was as snug as a kitten's pocket, a little kiss.

BOOK THREE: TRUDI

Trudi wasn't really Milly's maid. She was a friend helping out while the real maid's ankle healed, and if Milly slipped some money into Trudi's coat pocket sometimes, that was because she understood she was keeping Trudi from making money somewhere else.

Mornings Ione and Ruby and Tamar took the schoolbus to high school in town. They managed for themselves. They acted so sure that Trudi had nothing to teach them about how to dress or act. She guessed they were right. They were way ahead of her. They even knew how to get money out of Earl for clothes and lunches. She was sort of scared of them. They reminded her of ritzy girls she'd gone to school with and been scared of. But Earl Junior still let her take care of him, had no choice. She packed his lunchbox and made sure his fly was zipped, made sure he caught his school-bus clean and fed. She knew he would turn from her soon—he was looking more like Earl every day.

Trudi left her own house in a mess—whenever she started to clean it, she had to stop and cover her face with her hands and gasp for air. It felt like a swamp where she would get lost, or a big wave that would drown her. She was just through with that house. She had no heart for it. As Ada would say, she'd had it up to *here*.

Nice Barney had fixed up a rusty old 1934 Chevy for Trudi. It had been in a wreck and its doors didn't fit any more, and it shimmied if you went faster than thirty. But it was as good as money of her own for making her feel like a new woman. About all it could do was get her to Barney's every day and back again by the time Earl Junior's yellow bus brought him home, but that was enough. She wasn't spoiled or fussy. She loved that car. It took her to Barney's.

At Barney's, all the things Trudi couldn't stand to do any more were fun again. She even enjoyed sorting and rolling the millions of socks. The drawers looked like panfuls of bright biscuits. Maybe everybody should do somebody else's work and nobody would get sick of anything. Or maybe there was more to it than that, maybe you had to be helping someone you were very fond of and very sorry for, who had helped you a lot when you were at your wit's end, and who was still helping you all he could in spite of being so sad. Sometimes she just wished she could gather Barney up and rock him in a huge rocking chair.

One noon he came in for lunch actually whistling and she was so relieved in his behalf, until she remembered the words that went with that tune. It was a carol: " 'Fear not,' said he, for mighty dread had filled their troubled mind."

A little at a time Barney told her what the mighty dread was about, a hint now and then, but he was so loyal to Milly he couldn't bring himself to tell it all. Not that Trudi needed to be told: he was living in dread of losing his home. She saw Milly's clothes in the guest room, the guest bed slept in. She saw Milly every morning leave to work on that little shanty they all pretended was for Lil and her little boy, like anybody did that for a maid.

The Chevy got Trudi to Ada's, too. Ada was a waitress again and tired a lot, but she was always glad to see Trudi. Ada's house had started as one room, and then kitchen and bedrooms got added on all sides of that one room. The living room windows just looked into other rooms instead of outdoors. Still Ada had housewife thoughts about her house and had made a home of it. It was cozy. She compared and compared before she decided on living room curtains.

One day Trudi and Ada were talking at the very dining room table Ada had stood on to paint the ceiling. Ada's feet were in a pan of hot water.

"Just tell me this, Ada. Does anybody do that for a maid?"

"No, nobody does," Ada said.

"Well, what's it about then?"

"It's about how Lil's not the maid. She's the lady's lover," Ada said with her little impish look, settling back to enjoy Trudi's reaction.

"My God! Oh, my God!" Trudi cried, as shocked as though she didn't somehow already know.

"Oh, so what?" Ada said. She did like to pretend to be worldly, not born yesterday, not fazed by anything. "Come on," she said. "As sins go, it's pretty innocent. They can't make babies. They can't give each other VD."

"She's a *mother!* They're *both* mothers!"

"That never made anybody a saint so far."

"Poor Barney! Poor Barney!"

"He's had his fun. It's Milly's turn. It's about as wicked as playing cards. I'd put it somewhere between Bingo and cards."

"If I didn't know you better, I'd think you've got no morals."

Ada just grinned. She got such a kick out of kidding Trudi.

*****

Barney started coming home late for lunch, after the children had eaten and gone back to school. At first Trudi wasn't sure what he had in mind, but she soon realized he just needed somebody to talk to and she stopped feeling funny about being alone in the house with him. He just needed to be around somebody that liked him, besides his children, who certainly liked him—adored him. He needed to be around a grownup that liked him, besides his mechanics. He needed to be around a woman that liked him.

"I wish you'd stop waiting on me and sit down and eat," he said once, so after that they ate together. It was so hard to believe he was Earl's brother that she gradually came to forget. Barney became just a plain man that liked to be with her, a real first. He had as much reason as Earl to be a snob, in fact exactly the same reason, but he wasn't a snob at all and he never made her feel like a Child of Nature or a Peasant Lass. He was as smart as Earl, probably— though it was hard to tell because he never used big words— but he never made her feel dumb. He made her feel it was nice to be near her.

One day he pushed his chair back as usual, saying, as usual, "Well, back to the old rat race," stood up as usual, but hesitated and then came over to her and kissed the top of her head. Such a light touch, such a short little breeze from his breath, to give such a tingle! "Your hair smells nice. It shines," he mumbled, so awkward she had to laugh, and the next day when he was starting around the table to kiss her again she looked at him and tipped her face up. His kiss was so shy and awkward that she had to laugh again, and then he laughed too and seemed to remember he was a wicked sailor and gave her a big firm wet toothy tonguey kiss that didn't actually feel as good as the little light touch on her scalp had felt, but she liked it better because it meant more. As a feeling, it belonged somewhere between Bingo and cards, but as a meaning it was up beside murder and envy.

Naturally they soon wanted more, and as Trudi asked Ada, why shouldn't they? Didn't Earl do it all over town, even with Milly? With everybody except Trudi? Wasn't Milly a terrible wife who wouldn't do it with Barney or cook or clean and was queer to boot? Hadn't Trudi and Barney done everything possible to be good and faithful mates? Had they left any stone unturned?

Ada said, "Just shut up and do it."

"Would we ever do such a thing except they're so awful?"

"Just do it because you want to. Because you like each other. They don't have to be awful to give you an excuse."

Maybe not, but Trudi felt better knowing Earl and Milly were awful.

At first Trudi felt like a virgin again, but as time went on and more and more happened, she saw there was no "again" about it. She had been a virgin all along, despite all those babies coming out. Nothing worth mentioning had ever gone in, until Barney's big solid rosy tinkler, which he actually let her look at and play with. She had a lot of fun making it grow and ungrow, seeing if she could grow it up to his belly button (not quite), watching that funny little bag with its two plums inside (did Earl have one of those?) wrinkle and move by itself. And once Barney convinced her that he wasn't having fits and wasn't dying, she liked the rest of what happened, too. Liked it a lot. Loved it. Wished for it night and day.

But, strange to say, the best part was none of that. The best part was how Barney's face, every day, all day, was calm and sweet and his footstep springy. His nice white smile came popping out really often. He said he had to control himself or he'd be smiling like some sappy song-and-dance man all the time. And he whistled like all the birds of paradise busting loose at the same time, cheery tunes, no mighty dread. It all made her wonder what the world might be like if everybody could have a good love life. It even, somehow, made her see why Milly felt love was a matter of life and death, though why anyone would turn up her nose at Barney and go chasing after a woman was still a mystery. Trudi was not much interested any more in solving the mystery and certainly not in undoing it. Anything that brought her so much good should stay like it was and keep on. Milly's craziness began to look like God's Plan.

Trudi did have a few fears. One was that Milly would come to her senses and want Barney back, now that he was his beautiful real self again. Who wouldn't? Another fear was that Milly would change her mind about letting Barney and Trudi meet in the wonderful little house. Milly had worked so hard to make it into a love nest for Lil, and it was Barney and Trudi who romped in it every evening. Milly and Lil had to stay in the big house until almost midnight, and even when they could go to the little house they had to be quiet and careful because of Jack. Milly might begin to think Barney should stay with the kids sometimes.

Usually Trudi avoided Milly, but one day the Chevy added a new klunk to its regular noises and Trudi had to take it to Sunup Motors. There she found Milly *and* Barney *and* Earl practically standing in line, like they had arranged themselves on purpose to accuse Trudi of something. Then Barney, looking very cute and sexy in his greasy coveralls, took the Chevy into the shop and Earl went into the showroom, which still had no cars to show because they were snapped up so fast, and Milly went into the office, which had glass walls and was about as private as a Zyglo Line. "Come in, Trude," Milly said. She shut the door behind Trudi.

Trudi didn't know where to look. She just hoped nobody in the garage could read lips.

"You're looking bushy-tailed these days," Milly said.

Did love show on Trudi the way it did on Barney? Had she become beautiful too? Love, she noticed, was certainly showing on Milly.

"Uh, yes," Trudi said. "I've been feeling all right."

"There's a lot of that going around," Milly said.

"Uh, yes, I, uh, wondered what you thought about that."

Milly said, "I don't seem to mind."

"You look like you don't, but you still might."

"I've been paying attention to myself, and I think I can say I'm not jealous. I mystify myself. I mean, I may or may not love Barney, but there's no doubt that I love you."

Trudi had to gasp, with pleasure and embarrassment and relief. "I love you too," she mumbled and fled to the showroom where she grabbed up the first magazine she came to, and read it even though it was brainy, boring *Reader's Digest*.

The trouble with the showroom was that Earl was in it. She kept her nose glued to *Reader's Digest* but he must have figured she was faking. He came over and butted in, something he would never have let *her* get away with.

"Well, parapathetic one, you have alit," he said.

She put her finger on the line she was reading and tapped her foot. When Earl did that, you were supposed to shut up and go away, but it didn't work both ways. He never was fair.

"I appreciate your finding a minute for me in your busy schedule," he said.

She tapped both feet and put on a very cross expression, for all the good it did.

"I understand the maid's getting the cast off her ankle tomorrow. May we at the Old Homestead look forward to the resumption of certain amenities, vis à vis clean sheets? A path through the chaos? An acutal meal on the table?"

"The girls can do it," Trudi said without looking up.

"They have been doing as well as anyone could do whose mother has never taught them the merest rudiment. In any case, it is not *up* to them. It is up to *you*."

"Can't you see I'm reading?" She threw *Reader's Digest* down and stood up. She went to the shop. She was glad the mechanics were all over the place, even though they kept her from talking with Barney, because they kept Earl from following her and going on with his nagging. She paced around until her car was ready. She was very upset. She hadn't known Lil's ankle was well. Staying home was too dreadful to consider. The very idea made Trudi sick. If it hadn't been for Earl Junior she would never have gone home. It was time to start the restaurant.

* * * * *

Trudi and Ada rented a place that was narrow and not really so very long. It was fully equipped with a counter and a row of red-plastic-topped stools and a coat rack and a gas grill with a hood over it and a refrigerator with coils on top. The people who ran the place before had evidently left in haste, pausing only to take the money. There were beards of mold in the refrigerator, the grill hood and fan were clogged with grease, and so on. Ada decided to keep her waitress job, to make a little more money, while Trudi scrubbed everything. "While you dung it out," is what Ada actually said.

Trudi enjoyed the scouring. She enjoyed anything that wasn't at home. Nothing but scouring powder would cut the grease. The ceiling alone ·took two days. It was white-painted tin with fancy lumps and bulges shaped like vines and lilies and women's faces. It sure held the dirt. While she was up on the ladder, she would have settled for plain and flat, but afterward she realized that ceiling was the most wonderful she had ever seen. She looked up at it so much that Ada thought she was praying and told her to quit worrying.

In a couple of weeks, Trudi had the place as clean as it would ever be. She thought it was ready for business, but Barney said the health department had to inspect it and that she and Ada had to have physicals and chest X-rays. Trudi had a real tussle with herself not to hate Barney for that bad news. "It's not his fault, it's not his fault," she kept repeating, but she could have hit him. Hadn't the war been about dictatorship? What was the government's big idea, telling people if they could start a business or not? Kill Hitler one place and he pops up in your own backyard.

But all the dreary legal things did get done. Ada told her boss to take his job and shove it. Barney showed up with a surprise gift, a professionally painted sign: TRUDE & ADA'S, beautiful even though he got Trudi's name wrong. Milly brought one of those new split-leaf philodendrons that cost five dollars a leaf. It had seven leaves and a wide red ribbon across it that said GOOD LUCK. It looked just right on the ledge of the big sparkly-clean window. Murray and Rusty climbed around the front stringing up bunting and a GRAND OPENING sign. Betty made chef hats out of paper.

It was so heartwarming to have help from Barney's Sunup children when Trudi's own Sunup children, especially Ione, were mainly embarrassed, worried that the la-de-da Sunup name might be sullied by this shabby, hopeless little hot-dog stand. That's what they kept calling it even though it wasn't. They seemed to be picturing a tent at the county fair. Trudi had given up caring what they thought. She had no way of pleasing them. Back when she had given them every drop of her time and strength and love, they had not been pleased either. It was not in their nature to be pleased with her, or to be not pleased with Earl, who could hardly tell them apart. Any little fault he might have, like drinking, was something she drove him to.

Tamar said Earl Junior was growing up all wrong, a little savage, and took him under her wing. "He's a child of nature," she said. Trudi knew where that came from. Would the children have respected her if Earl had? Tamar was bent on making a real Sunup out of Earl Junior. She was fifteen and did, actually, have a motherly streak in her. She corrected his grammar and table manners, she hit him when he played with himself, she taught him to dance, she gave him nickels. She bought him clothes. She took his coffee away from him and gave him a boiled egg for breakfast. She read *Modern Parent* magazine.

"Leave him be. Stop fussing at him," Trudi said. She believed a child had a right to some leeway, some secrets. But he loved the attention and the nickels. To him, those pretty, grown-up, busy sisters had always seemed like movie stars. Sometimes he looked a little sheepish, like he knew he should side with his own mother, but he also seemed to expect Trudi to understand that he had to know which side his bread was buttered on and look out for Number One.

* * * * *

Trudi spent her evenings with Barney in the little house, wheeled home late, moved the unsorted laundry from the couch to Earl's chair, slept on the couch, left early. Every day Earl threw the laundry back to the couch, but folding it never seemed to cross his mind. It crossed hers. She just wouldn't. She had *done* that.

One night late she was doing the wash. That much she still did because she needed clean clothes herself and why not do everything while she was at it? Not to would be wasteful. Usually the machine's kerchug said Bar-*nee!* Bar-*nee!* but this night it said watch *out!* watch *out!* and first Earl and then everybody came stumbling to the kitchen, groggy with sleep and grouchy, spoiling for a fight, really ganging up on her.

"Do you have to run that damned thing in the middle of the night and keep us awake?" Earl yelled.

Trudi kept on feeding the wringer and said nothing. Watch *out,* watch *out!*

The girls stood clinging to him. They were getting too big for that sort of thing. They were tall, and even when sulky and grouchy, like now, so beautiful. They touched her heart, and the sight of poor little Earl Junior almost brought her to tears. He was clinging to Tamar, when he knew very well he should be sticking up for his mother.

Trudi's not answering made Earl even madder, but anything she might have said would have too.

"Do this in the *daytime!*" he yelled and stomped over to the electric cord hanging down from the ceiling and unplugged the washing machine. How dumb! What good did that do? Now there was a towel stopped mid-wringer and he was too mad to sleep anyway. She could have put the plug back in again, but she decided to hang up the wet basketful she already had.

Out into the cold night she went with her basket. There was a high cold moon. The air was so cold it made the cold wet clothes steam like they were hot. She had just begun pegging a sheet to the clothesline when she heard the lock click.

So *that's* what the washing machine had been trying to tell her.

Fortunately she had her car keys in her pants pocket. She had her house keys too, but going back in would be embarrassing. How do you look at somebody who's locked you out? How do they look at you? She gave the old car full-choke and floorboarded her. The engine roared a mighty roar. Her car, all things considered, was in A-number-one condition. Except for being cold, Trudi felt pretty good too. Owning something powerful was as good as being powerful yourself.

Then Earl was rapping on the car window. She tried to escape but the engine was still too cold. It killed. She started it again and rolled the window open just a crack.

"All right, Sarah Burn-hard," he said. "I think you've learned your lesson."

"I learned it. I already knew it. Never go out without your keys." She would have liked to rattle them at him, superiorly, but they were all dangling from the ignition.

"Gertrude," he began, firmly, patiently, kindly, but she didn't hear the rest.

The old car killed again twice on River Road, but at least she got Trudi down the driveway first, away from Earl, not with style, not very grandly, not without many jolts and sputters, but away, and then to Barney's.

Through the door's glass Trudi saw a pool of light with Barney sitting in it reading a book. She had never before known anybody who read actual books, not magazines. He looked so cozy. What a nice thing to do on a winter night while your wife's out making love with a woman. Somebody must have taken his mind off his wife. Somebody wonderful.

She almost rang the bell, but thought better of it. It would wake up the children. She tapped the glass lightly with her fingernail. He didn't look up, so she went in. No wonder he hadn't heard—he was playing one of his boring records, something with no tune and lots of fiddles jabbering, that you had to be very smart to like. When he felt the cold air she let in, he looked up.

"Trude, honey!" he said.

She dropped her coat to the floor and hurried to him.

He pulled her down to his warm lap, the world's best place to be.

"Oh, Barney," she whispered, "Earl locked me out."

"Well, that settles it. I haven't liked your being there anyway. You belong with me."

"I know I do."

"I don't quite see how to work it out, but we should be married."

She had expected to be thrilled when the time came, as she had known it would, for Barney to say that, but she felt just calm and natural. They simply belonged together. "I know," she said.

"I have to get some legal advice. I'll talk to my friend Rod tomorrow."

There were easy ways of doing things when you knew people, when you had friends named Rod. She knew she could leave everything to Barney, just do whatever he thought best.

"Meanwhile," he said, "you shouldn't be here. Until I get some information, we should be careful. Milly won't make any trouble, but Owl might."

"Oh, no, he'll be glad. He never liked me."

"Just in case, you should go to Ada's. I'm out of my depth here. I don't know enough. We don't want a mess." He stood up, lifting her too. He was so strong. He began to kiss her goodnight and pretty soon, like always, he was whispering wonderful mushy things between kisses, like, "We're going to be happy. I love you, I love you," which she was used to by now. Two months had wiped away a whole lifetime of thinking nobody would ever talk like that to her.

The record player shut itself off in time for them to hear footsteps on the porch and jump apart. Earl gave one rap and came in without waiting for an answer. "I've come for my wife," he said to Barney. "I thought you'd be here," he said to Trudi.

Barney said, "What's the big idea locking her out?"

"She told you that? That's family business, not yours. What's her big idea not coming back in when I told her to? It was a joke and she knew it."

"Nobody's laughing," Barney said.

"You want laughing? I'm laughing. Ha ha. This your coat, Gertrude? You didn't hang it up?" He picked her coat off the floor and held it open for her politely. She slipped her arms into the sleeves.

"Well, goodnight, Barney," she said.

Barney said, "Any time he locks you out, you know where to come. Are you going to Ada's now?"

Earl said, "You stay out of this. Mind your own business."

Trudi said, "No, I'll go back with him."

Barney said, "If you hurt her, I'll make it my business."

"I've never hurt her," Earl said. "Come on, Gertrude."

She followed his red tail lights home, followed his back along the unshoveled path, and then he held the kitchen door open for her as though to say, "Look, no locks," and she went in. The towel was still stuck halfway through the wringer. The washwater must have been ice cold. The children had gone back to bed.

"I really resent your scurrying around advising everybody of every little family contretemps we have," he began.

She got the gist. "I just told Barney. He's family."

Earl didn't listen. "Particularly when you don't see fit to tell the whole story or explain what the provocation was. Why do you never do your share for our family? Where are you every night?"

She thought laundry questions would come next and that she wouldn't have to say anything for a while, but he stopped there and waited.

"I want a divorce," she said. "I'm sick of all this."

"*You're* sick of it! *I'm* the one that's sick of it. I always have been. This marriage is torture and *you* want a divorce! You are solid brass!"

She kept still.

He said, "I've stayed with you, I've done my duty to you, through oceans of crap, and now *you're* sick of it. Well, you're not getting off that easy. You get a little hot-dog stand and suddenly you're *above* all this. Well, the Sunups don't get divorced. If we did, you'd have seen the last of me a long time ago."

"Barney's a Sunup, and he's getting a divorce."

That stopped Earl in his tracks. She could see him wondering if his dirty little you-know with Milly would come up in court. He thought he had such a poker face, so cool, but he was clear as glass.

While he was scared and swallowing, it seemed like a good chance to get away. She went to the living room and began throwing the laundry from the couch to Earl's chair. He followed her. She was getting paid back for ever wishing she could get his attention.

"I suppose it's Milly and her housekeeper," he said.

Even though Trudi was very tired and just wished Earl would shut up and go to bed, the chance to keep him worried, to give his nose one little twist, was too good to pass up. "Oh, no, I don't think it's that," she said. One little twist for old times' sake. "What could women do that would amount to anything?"

"Goddamn women get away with murder," Earl said jealously, like he hadn't got away with enough himself. There must have been something else he wished he could get away with. Then his scare came back and he forgot to envy women. "I wonder what it is then," he said, very by-the-way, offhand, the master poker player except for one little squeak.

"Don't worry," Trudi said, putting a sheet on the couch. "Barney knows the right people. He can keep everything hushed up."

She went to the bathroom to undress and put on her flannel nightgown. He was sitting in his chair on top of the laundry when she came back. She ignored him, set her alarm clock, and curled up shivering under the quilts, waiting for her body to warm the cold sheets. Next winter she and Barney would warm a bed together.

"When did you and Barney get so buddy-buddy?" Earl asked. "What's going on here?"

"Earl, tomorrow's the grand opening. I'd like to get a little bit of sleep."

"I'd like to know what's going on here."

For answer, she gave him a soft snore, set, she hoped, at just the right level to seem like the real thing. He would have seen right through a big loud snore. After about ten soft snores, he turned off the light and went away. She stayed awake just long enough to smile.

* * * * *

Trudi was at the restaurant door getting out her key when Ada came up behind her, reached under her arm, and unlocked the door. It was six in the morning, still dark, and another cold windy one, but there they both were at exactly the time they had agreed on. Ada was like Barney, a partner you could count on. They put on their hairnets and the chef hats Betty had made for them, put on long white canvas aprons. Trudi started the coffee. Ada heated up the grill. The window steamed up. Soon the whole place was warm and fragrant. At seven Ada raised the shade on the door and they were open for business.

"Stand back, here they come!" Ada cried. "Back, you

crazy bastards, back!" and Trudi smiled politely, trying to believe someone really would come.

Who came first was dear Barney. He was careful, merely friendly to Trudi, though the sight of him made her grin ear to ear. "How's business conditions?" he asked Ada. "Have you had a customer yet?"

Ada pulled herself up very straight, like a soldier. She held out her egg turner like a rifle presented for inspection and then rapped the handle down smartly on the counter. "No," she said, "but I's weddy."

The menu was short and simple. Hamburgers, cheeseburgers, chili, french fries. Keep it simple and keep it good, was what Ada had learned by being in the food game. A new restaurant always gets a run of business at first. If you're good, you can keep it. There was only one choice for breakfast. It was from a recipe that had been in Ada's family for a long time: a gently fried egg, a thin slice of ham and a slice of melted cheese stacked on a toasted hamburger bun with a sprinkle of the chives Ada grew in pots. They called it Egg Ada. "It's wonderful," Barney said and had another. He insisted on paying. If he didn't pay, he wouldn't count as their first customer.

"If you don't mind a suggestion," he said, "a metal ring to cook the egg in would keep it from spreading. I could make you some."

"Metal would taste," Ada said.

"I can make them out of stainless steel."

"Well sure. Well thanks," Ada said, and when he left she said, "So that's your Barney," impressed. She said Barney was the best guy she'd ever seen. "Does he have a brother? Oh, yeah, I guess he does." She began to agree that Milly must be nuts. Trudi's ribs clanged and throbbed with pride. Her chest felt like a gong.

* * * * *

Earl started going to a crazy-people doctor. He wanted Trudi to go too, "to save the marriage," but she was too busy and anyway not interested. Every night when she got home, he was there, not drinking. He even finished the load of wash he had unplugged, and dried it and folded it, along with what was on the couch—or maybe the girls did that, but they wouldn't have unless he told them to. Trudi had to laugh. He acted like he was doing her a favor when he took care of his own stuff, and her heart should melt.

She would come in at midnight, really tired from the restaurant, which was succeeding maybe too well, and from a quick meeting with Barney, and there'd be Earl wide awake, chatty, gabbedy-gabbedy, my God, when all she wanted was to go right to sleep. While she got her clothes ready for the next day, he'd be watching her with sad sloppy eyes, saying the same things he'd said before. "June could really help you," he'd say. June was his doctor, but not a real doctor so it was all right to call her June. She was a Counsellor. "June could really open your eyes. She's certainly opened mine. I know now the reason I never initiated lovemaking. I was afraid you'd rebuff me."

That got a laugh out of Trudi the first few times he said it. If there was anything Earl didn't have to fear in the old days, it was that she'd say no. Remembering how much she had wanted him embarrassed her, but she remembered in spite of herself:

It had been so long. He must have some juice stored up. Men have to get rid of it like pee-pee, don't they? He was reading the paper, in a not very bad mood. The house was orderly and pleasant. The children were asleep. Gertrude— she was still dumb Gertrude then—settled herself on the floor between his knees, pretending to feel confident and natural. Hadn't he said a less heavyhanded approach might be more effective? He tried to clamp his knees together, but she had been too quick for him. "Oooh, what's this?" she squealed girlishly, finding the tag of his zipper. She slid the zipper open one tooth at a time, click click click, squealing, "Oooh, I wonder what's inside?"

"Grow up, Gertrude, you're not Shirley Temple," he said without lowering his newspaper.

Whenever she remembered times like that, she cringed. Her whole body blushed with shame. Why couldn't she forget?

But at least while she remembered, there was no danger that she'd feel sorry for Earl or give in to him, poor Earl who was trying so hard, who needed her so much, who was after her all the time, even in the morning, no matter how many times she said no. How come he didn't leave her alone if he was so afraid of no? He'd better ask June that.

"I married too young," he kept saying nonstop. "I was a late maturer, through no fault of my own. Some people just are. Einstein flunked second grade. I thought you trapped me. June has helped me see I was trying to hurt my father. I thought I needed somebody gorgeous that the boys would envy me for. Now I see you're the only one for me. You can't hold it against me, what I thought when I was young and foolish." He followed Trudi from room to room without pausing to catch his breath. "June could help Milly too. She doesn't have to be like that. You'd be amazed how common sense can help a problem. June could help Barney. I don't know what Barney's up to. I do know he always took everything of mine. He took my mother, he took my father, he took my jackknife. He didn't care the blade was broken just so he could take something of mine. You wouldn't let him take you away, would you, Gertrude? I don't have to let him have the love of my life, do I?"

Barney's lawyer friend had said not to tell Earl anything just yet. Trudi was so tempted to tell him that she was afraid she'd let it slip out if she said anything at all. To be safe, she never answered. Earl could guess all he wanted to, but unless she told him he wouldn't know. He must have felt he was talking to the wall but he didn't stop. He was like a Victrola with just one record. Put his needle down anywhere and he would say, "All I do is love you and love you and love you, and all you do is don't care and don't care and don't care."

Inside, she was laughing and laughing and laughing. She had never known people were so funny.

* * * * *

Barney began to look strained and worried. Trudi was afraid to ask him why because she thought he'd say she was too busy, these rushed little frantic meetings weren't satisfying him, he wanted to play and laugh the way they had before, she should give up the restaurant. And every bone in Trudi's body knew that without money of her own she would soon be Gertrude again.

But he looked so bad so many nights in a row that finally she had to ask him why. They were sitting at the table instead of in bed—it had come to that. He said pay him no mind, everything would work out somehow, and he didn't want to worry her. As though having the happiness go out of his face wouldn't worry her!

"Well," he admitted, "it's Milly."

He said he had just assumed that he and Trudi would keep the kids, and come to find out Milly was assuming all along that she and Lil would. It had never occurred to him she would want to. Motherly she was not, and the kids lived their own lives like little adults, which was probably all right in a way, but a child is entitled to a childhood and warm family times to remember, like they'd have with him and Trudi. Swimming, picnics, family hikes, camping trips, like that. Instead of just running around with their own friends or reading. Well, when Milly found out what he thought, she went to pieces, but he held out, saying she must understand it wouldn't be good for the kids to grow up in a lesbian household, and Milly pretended to see nothing wrong with that. It was good enough while he was in the Navy, wasn't it? That was different, he said. That was exactly the same, she said. She said she simply could not bear to leave her children, especially since she'd be with Lil's little boy and doing for him what she hadn't been able to do for her own. Barney stood his ground—he felt he had to for the sake of the kids—and Milly sobbed and went to bed and covered up her head and hadn't, at least while Barney was around, been up since. She kept saying from under the quilts, "I can't, I can't," in a dull, crazy voice. Once he had even tipped the bed up to roll her out, but she clung to it and stayed in. She was, he said, like a laboratory rat that had been shocked so often it couldn't jump any direction any more. He was thinking of asking Earl for the name of that counsellor.

So that's what the matter was.

Barney said the simple, hushed-up divorce was looking impossible. But everything would be all right, he said, because Milly, under it all, was a fair and honest person who loved her children and would do what was best for them.

"I hope you agree I'm doing the right thing," Barney said.

Trudi said, "Well, I can see both sides. She'd feel too guilty."

"Are you going to have fits of guilt if you leave your kids with Owl?"

"Well, mine don't like me. They're ashamed of me. But it's not like that with Milly. Honest, she'd feel too guilty. She's not putting it on."

"I'd feel guilty if I left them in such a weird household."

"They got along all right. They really did."

"They could end up funny like Milly."

"Oh, is that how she got funny?"

"Of course not. You should see her family. They're so normal. They're like a joke they're so normal."

"Then maybe there wouldn't be any harm. I mean, if that's not how a person gets funny."

"Trude, don't you want them? I thought you'd want them."

How could she run a business and take care of a houseful of children? Would he expect her to give up the restaurant? Leave Ada in the lurch? Not have money of her own? She loved him in every way, but did she love him enough for that?

"Of course I want them," she said carefully. "But I don't have my heart set on it."

"You don't?"

"Not really," she said, wondering if it would be her turn now to cry and cover her head.

He scared her by staying quiet, staring into his cup. He kept starting to say something and then thinking better of it. Just when she was on the verge of giving in, he said, "What would you think if I went back to school?"

She was so relieved she giggled. "You've been to school," she said.

"Do you know what a plant geneticist is?"

"Of course not."

"It's somebody who develops new kinds of plants. Like corn with two ears on a stalk instead of one, or rust-resistant wheat, or apple trees that bear every year and like that. And it's what I'd like to do." Then, looking ashamed, like he was being too stuck up, he mumbled, "I'd like to do something worthwhile for the world."

"That's just wonderful," she said.

"The government's giving veterans a free education. It's my chance to start over."

"That's just wonderful."

"You really don't mind leaving the kids with Milly?"

"Honest, they're all right with her."

He picked Trudi up and danced her so her feet didn't touch the floor. He was so happy, singing a no-tune song that said yes they could do it, they could postpone the Malthusian doomsday (did she hear that right?), yes they could make two blades of grass grow where only one grew before, no more garage, no more smell of metal on his hands. The smell of metal, he sang, was the smell of war and he hated it like he hated Sousa marches, flags, uniforms, guns, fire, death, and taxes. His hands would smell of pollen, sunny fields, peace, and love.

Still hugging her, he said, "Of course, we could take the kids to East Lansing. But there's millions of veterans with the same idea. We might have to live in an attic."

"East Lansing?"

He held her at arm's length. "That's where it is. That's where you study plant genetics. At Michigan State."

"I can't go to East Lansing. I've got a business to run."

He looked stunned and hurt. "What did you think?" he asked. "What did you think?"

She had thought he meant an adult-education course at the high school, but she certainly was not going to admit that. "I didn't think you'd ask me to leave my business."

"We don't need it. We'll get by. The government's paying a living allowance, and Milly will have to buy out my share of the garage. We'll have enough."

"*I* need it."

"No you don't. You'll be my wife."

"It's my new start. I'm not smart like you. I can't make new apples. I have to do what I can do."

"Trude, darling," he said patiently, "you're not seriously comparing your little dinette to plant genetics?"

"No. Yes. Why shouldn't I?"

"I can help solve a great world problem. I can be part of something important. I can feed Africa and India and South America."

"I can feed Mrs. Maleska."

"One person."

Trudi ignored the tiny sneer he said that with. "Not just her," she said. "We've got lots of regulars now."

"Oh, Trude, stop it. There's no comparison."

"If Africa is important, Mrs. Maleska is important," Trudi said stubbornly, even though she was so weak with fear that she had to sit down.

Her fear was that she'd give in and become the old Gertrude again. It was so hard to be selfish and stick up for herself. In East Lansing would she look through Barney's pockets for coins?

He stayed standing. "It's a matter of scale," he said. "A million Mrs. Maleskas are more important than one Mrs. Maleska. You can see that."

While Trude was trying to decide whether to admit she could see that, he began to rattle the keys in his pocket. He stood there tall and reasonable and patient and rattled his keys. Oh, no, not Barney. Please, God, not Barney too.

For him the argument seemed to be over. He had her stumped, so what else was there to talk about? He looked at his watch and said, "We've got time for a quick one." She knew from Ada that men thought they could be as mean as they pleased at nine and tumble you at ten.

"I'm tired," she said. "I have to go." And she went, leaving him to think what he liked. He could even, for all of her, think oh, no, not Trude, please God, not Trude too.

Why couldn't he call her Trudi like she'd asked him to?

* * * * *

Trudi always loved looking the length of the restaurant when the stools were full of people. It looked specially snug and nice today, as if to deny that it was unimportant. Snow falling outside. The radio playing cheery songs and ads (Ada said people, especially people with false teeth, wanted some kind of background noise while they ate, and they didn't care if it was an ad as long as it covered their clicks and slurps). The place was really cheery and happy, good-smelling, almost beautiful in its plain clean way. Ada was singing with the radio and producing Egg Adas six at a time. Nobody ever had only one.

Then the stools were empty and during the lull before the lunchtime rush, Trudi and Ada made everything clean and orderly again. Trudi loved the place then too—the ketchup bottles evenly spaced, standing on their reflections along the gleaming counter, the salt and pepper shakers beside them in couples. The egg man brought eggs. The bun man brought buns. They always made some joke, usually "Cold enough for you?" They were a lot of fun.

While Trudi was scouring the egg rings, she remembered that Barney didn't like metal. He shouldn't have made the rings then. Who asked him to? Anyway, they were hard to wash. You could cut yourself.

"What's the matter?" Ada asked.

"Did I say something was the matter?"

"Just shut up and tell me."

That was all the encouragement it took for the whole story to pour out. "But don't worry, I won't do it," Trudi said. "I love him, but he can't act like that. Like he's the only one with something to do."

"He's got a point. A million Mrs. Maleskas are more important than one Mrs. Maleska," Ada said. Sometimes her sense of fair play could drive a person crazy. Sometimes people should be on your side even if you're wrong.

"It's not *about* Mrs. Maleska," Trudi cried. "It's about *me*."

"Yeah," Ada said.

"I don't know how she even got into this. Who gives a damn about Mrs. Maleska?"

"Yeah."

"Why should I have to give up my independence just because I'm wrong? Just because I'm not smart enough to do something important? What's important? Who's important? What's so important about important?"

"Yeah," Ada said. "I always get a laugh in cemeteries."

"You've got some sense of humor," Trudi said, laughing in spite of herself. Ada was one of a kind.

"I mean, here's all these big tombstones that say 'Doctor Joe Blow' and like that, and shit, that's no doctor, that's mud."

A customer came in then. It was the first time Trudi was sorry to see a customer, but he did no harm after all because in half an hour, when he left, Ada picked up right where she had left off.

"If a tombstone wanted to say 'Here Lies a Great Lover,' I'd make an exception. I'd give it the benefit of the doubt," she said.

"Great lovers don't turn to mud, huh?"

"Well, I suppose. But it's a different kind of mud. It's sparkly."

"That's what Milly thinks. Love is all that counts, she thinks."

"I'm not the best of proof of it, but she's right."

"Not letting your friends down counts too," Trudi said. "If I went off to East Lansing I'd be letting you down."

"Oh, I'd get by," Ada said. "I'd get another partner."

"Who?" Trudi asked jealously, certain nobody could be as perfect as herself.

"Well, Persis for one."

"Persis! She thinks too much of herself."

"Not half as much as I think of myself," Ada said. "But I'd feel like a rat if you let Barney get away for my sake."

Trudi tried to picture Persis in the restaurant. Her mass of black-dyed hair. Her long painted fingernails. She'd have a line of smart remarks for the customers, but could that take the place of Trudi's steadiness and hard work?

"Just believe me," Ada said. "I know a lot of people in the profession. If not Persis, somebody else. Listen, you remember those two gals at Spragg's that got caught kissing?"

"Sure," Trudi said, offhand. Would Ada want to be alone with Trudi if she admitted she remembered them very well?

"They want to meet Milly and her girlfriend."

"Ada, you are not supposed to repeat what I tell you in private."

"Oh, come off it. You know I only tell where it does no harm. They want us to bring Milly and her girlfriend to their house for dinner. Think they'll come?"

"I'll ask."

* * * * *

Lil, looking not very friendly, looking like she'd been crying, let Trudi in. Jack was talking to his toy trucks on the kitchen floor. Lil said, "Milly's in bed. She's not seeing anybody. You want a cup of coffee?"

"She'll see me. I've got good news," Trudi said and started up the dear familiar stairs before Lil could stop her.

Lil yelled, "Milly, you've got company!"

"No!" Milly howled, but Trudi was beside the bed by then. The bedroom smelled of too much sleep.

"I can't," Milly said from under the quilt. "I'm sorry, I can't talk to you. I really can't."

"It's Trudi. Didn't Barney tell you? You can keep your kids."

Milly uncovered her face, which was blotchy and puffy, very un-Millylike. "Yeah?"

"Yeah. And you can have the garage, but he wants you to buy his share. We're going over to Michigan State to raise apples. *Better* apples. Because you're right—love is all that counts."

Milly sat up, laughing and hitting her head, saying, "Wow! Oh, wow! I've got to pee. I've got to tell Lil. I've got to brush my teeth. My mouth tastes like a sewer. Oh, wow!"

Funny the simple things people say when their life takes a sudden upturn. "Oh, wow!" was the last thing Trudi expected out of Milly.

Milly swung her legs out of bed and was up, naked, in one jump. Staying in bed hadn't sapped her strength. She looked stronger than ever, taking long fast steps to the bathroom, yelling, "Lil, it's okay. We're all set. Everything's okay!" Her big round butt had muscle in it. It was sort of too bad she disappeared so fast. She looked, yes, beautiful. She could choke you up.

Lil came running up the stairs, asking, "What do you mean? What happened?" Not sulky now. Peppy and laughing. Lovable. Behind her came Jack repeating everything she said.

He was trying to get into the bathroom, too, but Trudi stopped him by saying, "Do you know what lives in the hole in the big tree out front? A teeny-weeny family!" That got him. "A teeny-weeny boy named John just this big and a teeny-weeny daddy and mommy just *this* big, I mean two teeny-weeny mommies. At night they sneak in and drive your trucks."

She was almost out of ideas—she was down to buckets made of acorns—by the time the bathroom door opened and

Lil and Milly came out. Milly was all respectable in a blue flannel robe and smelled of mint. They looked like they'd never known a sad moment their whole lives long, like life to them was one long day in May.

Trudi said, "A couple of women want you and Ada and me to come to dinner. Okay? They live together."

"Sure," Milly and Lil said. It would have been a good time to ask for blood or money. They were in no mood to say no to anything.

"Me too," Jack said. "Me too."

Trudi said, "John and his friends always stay with a teeny-weeny babysitter. Come on, I'll show you their house."

She supposed Milly and Lil found something to do while Jack was outside.

* * * * *

That night Barney got to the little house first. When Trudi went in he grabbed her, quite roughly, and gave her a fierce kiss that bent her head back and took her breath away. That is, it blocked her nose, but she managed to wiggle one nostril free and then she liked it, a lot. She liked a certain bossiness in him sometimes, as long as he wanted what she wanted. Maybe she *was* a beagle bitch, like Earl used to say. "Take your clothes off," Barney muttered. That kind of bossiness she liked, though she hoped that later on, when their life reached a different stage, he might be willing to see how he liked necking and cuddling a while before they took their clothes off.

But tonight he'd been waiting and he was ready. She had thought he might be, from missing last night, so her diaphragm was in. Lucky it was. He was on her and in her before they could get to the bed, pumping away with his eyes rolled back in his head, just white slits showing, kind of spooky until you got used to it, but kind of enviable too—

imagine being lost like that in a safe way you know you can get back from. Not that she didn't get lost too, in her own way. When he butted against a certain place inside her she forgot the floor was cold and hard, forgot it was dumb to be uncomfortable while the bed was so near, pushed her hips up to point him to the right place, moaned and sobbed, but she could have stopped any time and she could always see. For him, it was like a big animal picked him up and shook him. He was in its power.

Then they got into bed and he kept his thumb high up inside her touching the place while she hugged him close and warm with arms and legs. This was the best part, but the other had to come first. She could have a hundred sweet little comes this way and a conversation too. The comes just happened, like a sudden wind moving tree leaves, and then the conversation went on.

He said, "You went to see Milly today. I'm surprised she let you in."

"She didn't. I just went. It's great being the one that brings good news. It made me feel so good to be right there and see the change come over her. But you should have told her everything was all right. She had to suffer an extra day."

He laughed. He was so soft now, ready to laugh, a rag doll. "I didn't know, myself. Why did you tell her before you told me?"

"Well, we agreed about the kids. You could have told her that much."

"It was so awful last night. I didn't know up from down. I didn't know what to tell myself, much less her. I wasn't even sure you'd come tonight."

"But you shaved, just in case," she said. She loved his cheeks when they were new-shaved. Couldn't keep her mouth off them.

"I was so pissed at you I nicked myself."

"I know. I was too, at you."

"That's what pissed me. There shouldn't be all this resistance. A man's supposed to make the decisions. That's the way it's been since time immemorial. It's nothing personal. That's just the way it is."

"A man's supposed to smell like you do, too," she said.

"He hopes he's a good man and makes wise decisions, but even if he's not he has to do it. That's what being a man *means*. A woman recognizes that and doesn't make it harder for him."

While his thumbtip was touching the place, she didn't care what he said. "That's what you've been thinking all day," she said, kissing his fragrant cheek. It was cute of him to have speeches and arguments running in his head all day, just like her. She wondered if Earl Junior did, too—if he was thinking like Barney when he climbed a pile of sand and yelled, "I'm the king of the mountain!"

Barney said, "It's like being the captain of a ship. A man has to be *responsible*. Otherwise there's chaos and the ship is lost."

"I see. And the sailors, that aren't the captain, they're like women."

He tightened up, lost his softness. "No, no!" he said. "They're men. They're real men."

"Sorry," she said. She didn't want to make him mad again. She just wanted to keep him talking so she could feel the rumble of his deep voice in his chest. It didn't matter what he said. She pushed her place down against his thumb to bring on a come and take his mind off her misstep.

Then he was soft again, rumbling on with what he'd been thinking all day: "What if we hadn't been able to get back together? The thought of having to go without you just killed me. I told myself the world's full of women, but how many real women? I've met bitches, and mannequins, and you. I could spend years looking for another you."

Trudi said, "You don't need another me. You've got the original."

He said, "I used to be afraid I couldn't love anybody but Milly. Where would I ever find anybody else like her? Then I loved you, and that showed me I didn't need somebody like her. I didn't have to put up with her. I could have a real wife and a pleasant home and good sex and good meals and not have to look through the laundry basket for clean socks."

"Umm," she said, glad he couldn't look into her mind and see the socks and underwear heaped taller than her tall couch arms. She didn't want to spoil his good mood by mentioning that she would, of course, get a job in East Lansing and might possibly neglect socks sometimes.

Lazy and smily, they heated water and washed the sex juices away. Too bad this perfect love nest had no bathtub. Too bad sex was such a mess. How did people manage who made love in cars?

"By the way," Trudi said, "I won't be here tomorrow night. I'm going out to dinner with Milly and Lil and Ada."

"What?"

"It's at some women's that live together."

"What?"

"They want to meet Milly and Lil."

"So what? What's that got to do with you?"

"I'm curious," she said, and his tinkler, which had been limp and pale, satisfied, asleep, a mere cigar butt, came untucked and stood up tall and red. He pushed her against the kitchen wall. It was a terrible position. It wouldn't do as a regular way, but it was exciting as a change.

And now she knew what to say if ever he didn't feel like making love.

* * * * *

It felt funny, four women in a car. Cars are supposed to have a man, a woman, and children in them. It felt funny being in the backseat with Ada, side by side like mates. Between the two halves of the front-seat back, Trudi could see that Lil's hand was on Milly's thigh while Milly drove. That felt funniest of all, but funnier was to come.

The house of Those Women, for instance, was just like anybody else's: brown-shingle siding on the outside; blue overstuffed couch and chair and glass-topped end tables that came as a set from Sears; lace curtains; on the walls pictures of sunsets and windmills and those dogs that rescue people; high-school graduation pictures and baby pictures on the piano in silver frames; a basketful of yarn; coleus spindly and green from lack of sun, philodendrons and wax begonias doing fine, a poinsettia left over from Christmas just barely hanging on, two leaves and a stem. Their house should be different. Why wasn't it different?

And Those Women, whose names were Dot and Fran, were ordinary too. Wasn't one supposed to be mannish? Why were they both wearing lipstick and calico bib aprons? Their hair was curled, even. They were both on the plump side, but that was not unusual. They both wore slacks, but who didn't these days? Trudi bet they sang in a church choir.

They weren't a bit the way they were on that terrible-wonderful morning when the Zyglo Line walked them to their car. Trudi would not have recognized them. So beaten-down and grayish that morning, so chipper and laughy and pink tonight, excited about meeting their Own Kind, proud of their pretty home, so welcoming, so nice, so comfy.

Dot (the short one, the one more like a dot) was passing out crackers and Velveeta. Fran was in the kitchen. "Sweetheart," Fran called, "where's the corkscrew?"

That was the strangest, and Trudi snuck a look at Milly to see how she was taking it. Milly's face was tipped up, mouth up at the corners and a little open, eyes somewhat glassy. Trudi knew Milly was hearing the angels sing.

For the first time, Trudi understood how lonely Milly had been all those years.

Trudi hoped Milly would' get to know so many women who called each other sweetheart that they'd get to be old-hat, a so-so story.

Dot said, "Soup's on. It's nothing fancy. Just a family meal. You're getting the luck of the pot."

"We have wine every night. That's why we always know where the corkscrew is," Fran said.

Dinner was meatloaf, baked potatoes, a salad. "Good, good," they all said. Men, even Barney, thought if they ate something that was praise enough.

"Is the salad all right?" Dot asked.

"It's great," Ada said. The salad was lettuce, tomatoes, sliced cucumbers, and storeboughten French dressing.

"It's kind of experimental. We just tried different combinations till we found what we like best."

"You've got it, Dot," Ada said with her lovingest smile, not sarcastic. "Don't touch a thing."

Dot was a long-distance operator at the phone company. Fran clerked in a dry-goods store. "How did you find each other?" Lil asked. In church. Not a scary church. A Unitarian church—kindness and progress. A white-haired lady introduced them, saying, "I know you'll love each other." Fran talked Dot into joining the choir. (Aha!)

That all the good the past has had
Remains to make our own time glad,
Our common daily life divine,
And ev'ry land a Palestine

they sang in close harmony. Fran was alto, Dot soprano. Fran must be the man.

"Do you have neighbor problems?" Lil asked. No. Fran and Dot said hello, sure hot, sure cold. They were very busy. They never sat on the porch. Who'd believe they were too busy to chat if they did? If you must rock on the porch, make it the back porch. "And it's best to look like no man would have you. Look leftover, you know, but still like you share their values," Fran said. "Being fat helps."

"I'm getting you a case of Milky Ways," Milly told Lil. Lil didn't look quite leftover enough, but she could work on it.

Dot said, "People feel sorry for us. We've got such nice souls. Why do men only care for looks?"

Lil said, "I hate it when people are sorry for me. Even when my husband got killed, I hated people's pity."

"It's only fair. They feel sorry for me, I feel sorry for them. It evens out," Fran said.

Milly said, "Do you have other friends like us?" A few. Never enough. Everybody's so careful. But some women phoned after the scandal at Spragg's and said they were the same. They had become friends. A very silvery lining in a cloud that had looked hopelessly cloudy. Whooda thunk it?

After dinner Dot played old songs on the piano, *Camptown Races* and *Merry Oldsmobile* and so on, *Spanish Cavalier*, and everybody else beat time with tambourines or sticks or painted gourds and sang. Lil said, "You know where it says the Spanish cavalier stood in his retreat? When I was a kid, I thought a retreat must be some kind of long underwear."

It was absolutely the best evening Trudi ever had, bar none. Bar none. Bar really none. It almost, but not quite, made Trudi wish she'd had the nerve to be like those women back when Milly was giving her the chance to. But they still hadn't faced up to the question of what would become of them. There they were singing and laughing and having fun, a lot of fun, pretending the volcano would never blow up, the ax would never drop. In the end, some little mistake, somebody's suspicion, would get them—and they knew it. They must have made their heads go white inside.

* * * * *

One spring night Barney said his lawyer friend Rod had everything lined up and it was time to tell Earl. Trudi felt scared. Did she and Barney need to get married? Her name was Sunup already. Nobody in East Lansing would know the difference. But Barney said yes, they needed to be married. "There's nothing wrong with divorce," he said. "Society provides for it. Society recognizes it. It's perfectly legal, like marriage."

Then why did she feel so nervous?

"Just leave it all to me," he said, and she was glad to.

"Will you tell Earl, too?"

"Don't worry. I'll buy him," Barney said.

Earl, like always, was waiting for her on the back porch at midnight. "I married too young," he said. "I was a late maturer," and then Barney's car pulled in. "Here it comes," Earl said.

"Uh huh," Trudi said.

Barney's hair had apple blossom petals in it, like huge dandruff in the moonlight. He looked so funny, but he didn't know it.

"Owl, I think you've pretty much guessed everything," he said.

"Here it comes," Earl said.

"Milly and I are divorcing."

"Here it comes," Earl said.

"Uh, yes. You've got it." Barney took a deep breath and said, "Trude's divorcing you. We're getting married."

Earl sat down on the step and covered his face with his hands. "Oh, God," he moaned. "Oh, my God! How can something you already know be such a shock? How can it hurt so much?"

Barney said, "It's best this way. For everyone. For you, too. We all need a new start. We've all done too many unforgivable things."

"*You* have, *you* have," Earl said. "Speak for yourself.

You were always a sneak and a thief. You always had to have everything of mine. Everything went to hell when you got born. You know that, don't you, Gertrude? Trudi. You want to be called Trudi? All right, all right. I tried to give you your dignity by calling you by your proper name. But Trudi it is. Trudi, he only wants you because you're mine. You know that, don't you? He has followed me every step of his life cheating me out of what's mine. He got my jackknife. He got my record of *Mother Hasn't Spoke to Father Since*. He got my education. He got my inheritance."

What inheritance? Trudi knew for a fact that old Dad Sunup had died without a cent and that Barney sent money to Mom Sunup.

Barney said, "I've been wanting to make it right about the inheritance."

Earl wasn't listening. "He's a weasel," Earl said. "He thinks he can get away with anything if he smiles. He got Sunup Motors and I got that flyshitty grocery in Gray Oaks."

"I've been wanting to make that up to you," Barney said.

"This is how you make it up? By making it a clean sweep? Trudi, I've stood by you. Remember our beautiful babies? Remember the poor little blue ones? How many nights I broke down and bawled over them! How many nights we cried ourselves to sleep in each others arms!"

He really seemed to believe that. She opened her mouth to set the record straight, but Barney made a gesture that meant let him talk.

"We were two blundering children alone against the world. We made mistakes, but we saw each other through. We helped each other grow. When I lost my way, you lovingly called me back, guided me back. Trudi, Trudi, so much love can't die just like that. I know it's still in your heart. It's still in mine. Trudi?"

Had he lost his mind?

"Owl," Barney said, "I want to make it right about the inheritance. You know Dad was pretty down on his luck. He didn't leave much. I think if I transferred a thousand dollars to you, that would be fair."

Earl sat up straight and wiped his eyes. "All I ever asked for was justice," he said. "I would never hold anyone against her will. The children and I will see each other through. You wouldn't take the children?"

Trudi said, "Oh, no. They belong with you. They're just like you."

"You wouldn't take my job away?"

Barney said, "The garage goes to Milly. She says she'll keep you on. You're a very good salesman."

"Perhaps I'll learn to be content," Earl said, cheerful from the praise. "June says I try too hard. I ask too much of myself."

Then Earl and Barney and Trudi sat in a row on the step and Barney talked about what Rod had told him. The Constitution, Barney explained, said there could not be secret trials in the United States. That was because in olden days, kings could secretly try somebody alone in the night and have him executed and then pretend he had just mysteriously disappeared. So an open trial was a great and precious civil liberty. The founding fathers were wise and good to provide it, but luckily they never said a trial couldn't be quiet.

Rod had talked to the judge "in chambers," which probably meant in the back room, and told him that Earl was an alcoholic, a compulsive gambler, and a habitual adulterer.

"Now just a minute!" Earl said.

"That's not coming out in court. The judge will accept Trude's complaint of cruelty. But we have no intent to deceive him. He has to be satisfied that there are adequate grounds."

"I don't like it," Earl grumbled. "Does he know you two are going to turn right around and get married? Does he know that's what this is all about? Does he know you two are adulterers?"

"Yes, he knows that," Barney said. "Rod also told the judge Milly is a homosexual. The judge said that's not a problem that goes away and, yes, that marriage should be dissolved. Homosexuality won't go into the record. He'll accept a charge of cruelty from Milly too, and not ask too many questions."

That Trudi didn't like. "Milly's got some nerve saying you're cruel."

"It's just what's usual. It's a few nonsense syllables everybody accepts," Barney said.

"I think you should say Milly is cruel," Trudi said.

"No, that would be unusual. We don't want anything unusual."

* * * * *

From that night until the divorces, Trudi slept on Ada's couch. She missed, of all things, her tulips. They were spelling Sunup in thicker letters this year because the bulbs had doubled. They reminded her of so many things she had started with high hopes and good intentions, and they made her sad.

But she wanted to be reminded that she had been really sincere, had really tried to be a virtuous wife. "It's a very strange feeling to know that the name of what you're doing is 'adultery,' " she told Milly.

"I know," Milly said. "The name of what I'm doing is 'a crime against nature.' "

The divorces were scheduled for the very end of a beautiful spring day, blossoms everywhere. When Trudi got to the courthouse, the others were already there—Milly, Barney,

Earl, Ada, Lil, and the two lawyers—all dressed up and solemn, like for a funeral. They had been waiting on the tall stone steps for Trudi and when she came they all went inside and walked down a long stone hallway that smelled of paper, like school, to the stone and wood courtroom where some men were arguing about who was the rightful owner of some turkeys. A dusty-looking little man was writing everything down. Would he write down that Barney was cruel?

The judge could have been the bun man or a welder at Spragg's or one of Barney's mechanics or anybody. You couldn't tell by looking, except for his black outfit and high seat, that he was important and that his tombstone would say Judge.

The turkey people finished up and left. Milly, looking sad and clumsy in a dress—who would have guessed she even owned one?—went up front, swore to tell the truth, sat down, and immediately lied. Barney had beaten her severely on several occasions, she said. That is, she said yes when Rod asked if Barney had. The judge looked at her with such a tender look on his face, like he had fallen in love with her. Was he nuts or something? Then first Ada and then Lil swore they had seen Milly bruised on several occasions.

Next Barney and the other lawyer denied that Barney had ever hit Milly. The judge rapped with his mallet and said he found for the plaintiff (Milly) and gave her custody of the children, and Barney visiting rights. "Let the property agreement be made a part of the record," he said. The dusty man had written it all down.

Trudi's turn was next. She had made a new dress in the hope of making Barney proud of her, but she felt like a frump and the judge seemed cold. Had he guessed that she wouldn't have been able to tell him from a bun man? She swore yes, Earl had beaten her (the one thing he hadn't done) and Lil and Ada swore they had seen her bruised on several occasions. Earl and Rod denied everything. The judge found for Trudi and gave her the children (he didn't have to know where the children would be living). Rod handed out copies of the divorce decrees. The dusty man turned off the lights.

Out in the hall again, Barney said, "Now, Rod, this won't be in the paper, right?" Vital Statistics were the only interesting part of the paper. Births, deaths, marriages, divorces. Even Trudi read that much.

Rod said, "It definitely will not. Don't sweat it. You're home free. One of my clients is a doctor who got divorced without anybody's knowing it, and he's remarried and nobody knows that either."

Maybe being important was worthwhile after all, at least while you were alive.

* * * * *

Trudi and Barney got married on their way to East Lansing, in a little town they chose for its looks, in the office of a justice of the peace, with strangers as witnesses. There was no other way to do it without having attention paid, and luckily it was what they both preferred. They hated fuss.

Getting married the way runaway children do made them feel young, in a pleasanter way than when they were really young. "You were born an old man," his father used to tell Barney, making him ashamed on top of worried. Trudi said she had been too scared, too awkward, poor, and shy. Today they felt healthy and alive, the good way of being young. Imagine getting a chance to be young again in the middle of your life and do it better.

"What have you done to Michigan?" Barney marveled. "It's beautiful!"

Which it was, and Trudi suspected they could have seen

that anyway, even unhappy. It was hard to miss. The leaves were shiny, the grass was shiny and full of dandelions. The smell of flowering honey locust trees poured through the open car windows and rode along for miles.

Barney had already applied for married-student housing. He must have applied before she agreed to come with him, because he had made great progress on the waiting list. Even though the college was crowded with veterans who had lost too much time and didn't want to lose another minute, who were here for summer school and night classes and anything they could get, and had their families with them because love couldn't wait either, Barney came out of the housing office holding up a key. It was brand new and shiny like the grass.

They drove along a dirt road through acres of gray housetrailers and pregnant women until they found the right section and then they walked along a narrow wooden walkway to the gray housetrailer assigned to them.

"Oh, this won't do," Barney said. "No wonder we got it so fast. Everybody else passed it up. And we will too."

"You could at least look inside," Trudi said.

He unlocked the padlock. He bumped his head in the low doorway. "There's no bathroom. No water. I guess you go to the service house for all that. Look at this, a camp stove. You have to pump it. The refrigerator takes real live ice. I guess you go to the service house for that, too."

They went out and bought a newspaper and chased down For Rent ads all afternoon. The upstairses of Cape Cod cottages. One room, share bath and kitchen with the landlady. A garage not even finished inside, still with its big door. The whole world was coming to Michigan State at the same time. Somebody would rent those places. Would have to.

"But we don't have to," Barney said. "There's still little towns near by. Easy commutes."

"You'd have to take the car. I don't want to be stuck in a little town with no car."

"Would you rather live in that trailer?"

"Yes."

"It's like camping out. It's kid stuff. We're not kids."

"Sure we are," Trudi said.

That pleased him, but he still said no and no and again no, he would not live that way when he did not have to. "Don't you know the war was fought for hot and cold running water?" he asked, probably kidding. She started a smile that could go either way, depending.

They went to a hotel in Lansing and took a very fancy room. It had its own telephone and tile bathroom. Hotels had come a long way since the summer she emptied the Sunup chamberpots at Saugatuck and met Earl. Of course those pots were just for pee-pee in the night. There was a bathroom down the hall.

She wished she hadn't thought of Saugatuck. She was feeling too much like a maid already without that awful memory. She was ashamed of being willing to live in that trailer, ashamed of being afraid of the bell captain like he was still her boss. She was on the other end now, Mrs. Sunup not once but twice. Bell captains called her ma'am. She would have to learn to walk bosom-first like the real Mrs. Sunup and say, "My good man, the towels were not changed this morning. You will speak to the housekeeper? Thank you so much."

Barney was calling real estate people, who would charge, he said, the same as a month's rent for finding an apartment. He seemed to see nothing unreasonable in that, but it made her gasp. What did they *do* for all that money? "They keep the good places out of the want ads. They keep the riffraff from finding out about the good places," Barney said, like he thought that was worth any amount. She would not let herself feel hurt. He wouldn't have said that if he thought she was riffraff. He wouldn't have married her. He would apologize all over the place if he knew she minded when anything was said against riffraff. She had, as Earl put it, a natural sympathy with the servant classes.

"Yes," Barney said in a deep, important voice she didn't recognize. "This is Barney Sunup. I'm in the market for an apartment. . . . We'll need at least two bedrooms. Modern kitchen and bath, of course. What's the range on that? . . . That's quite acceptable. . . . Immediately. . . . Then I'll expect your call." He did it again, several times in a row, while Trudi watched him from the big soft bed. She was almost scared of him.

Then he went into the bathroom and when he came out, naked, he was her plain good Barney again, her plain good playmate and ever-horny boyfriend, not a bit like Earl. Getting married hadn't hurt a thing.

* * * * *

They got a wonderful apartment in Lansing. It was half of the first floor of a real mansion. Barney said houses like this had been built by millionaires to be family estates and family gathering places for countless generations, and then even the second generation, except sometimes one ancient daughter, hadn't wanted them. Sometimes the children couldn't afford them, but usually they simply didn't care. They sold the land to developers and then they didn't like the neighborhood. "Funny thing about America. The dynastic idea just never took hold here," he said. "Every generation starts over."

Trudi imagined that the millionaire who built their house was just like Dad Sunup, bossy and mean, but she pitied him anyway for the dream he couldn't make work. She was glad the house had somebody in it again that loved it. She loved her kitchen, which had been a solarium, a half-round glass room on the end of the house. Such light! She figured she could grow tomatoes and zinnias all winter. The rest of the apartment, despite being only a quarter of the house, went on and on. So many tall gorgeous rooms with carved mahogany doorframes and windowframes, windows down to the floor with wooden shutters that folded into the frames, molded ceilings not at all like tin, fireplaces framed in marble or mahogany, huge high closets with hangers on sticks because the poles were way up for hanging ballgowns. The bathroom faucets were shaped like swans and seagulls. The library became Barney's study. It had built-in mahogany shelves instead of walls, empty except for his few textbooks. His desk looked dinky and pitiful in such a room.

A house like this could give you ideas about countless generations. It should be full of children. It should have beautiful rugs. It should have furniture she couldn't imagine, not from Sears.

At first Barney helped her think and plan and shop. He had to study the decorating magazines, too. Nothing in his fancy childhood had been this fancy. But then he got so busy with summer school and trying to cram tons of new facts every day into a brain that was, he said, past the age of easy learning, that he stopped helping her. He gave her a household checking account. "Get good stuff," he said. "We're not kids. We're not camping. This is a serious home. Get a few good pieces we can add on to. I want a nice home."

She shopped alone and scared. Her riffraff background, her terrible taste, made her feel like a kid in the old bad way. Dumb.

She saw an easy chair she liked. Would he come look at it? "Honest, honey, I just don't have time. If you like it, I'll like it." She bought it. He hated it. It had been on special sale, no returns. There were shiny metal threads running here and there in the cloth. She hadn't noticed that in the store. And outside the store, the blue was too bright, almost turquoise. She wanted to pay for the chair out of what was left of her own money, since Barney didn't like it. "Don't be silly," he said. "You made a mistake. So what? It's not the end of the world."

But it sort of was. Maybe not of the world, but of her furniture shopping. "I'm too dumb to shop," she wept, and he came around the dinner table and patted her saying, "There, there, it's all right. You don't have to." When she stopped crying, he went back to his plate.

"Milly could do it," she said.

"Milly'd buy junk and fix it. She'd keep everything in an uproar. Half-fixed, unfixed, all in a jumble. She can't pass a second-hand store."

"Should I be like that?"

"God no! I hate mess. I hate discomfort. I want a simple life of work and meals and lovemaking. In a house that isn't coming undone all the time. I'm a very simple man. I want a simple woman like you who isn't above taking care of me and letting me get on with my work."

How could "simple man" sound so good and "simple woman" sound like simple shit? She would not be hurt. He had only said they were both equally simple.

He said, "I love it that you like to please me."

"Oh, yes, yes, I want to please you."

"That's what I first admired in you, your capacity for devotion. It was all wasted on Owl, but it's not wasted on me. I love knowing I can leave my whole private life in your hands and you'll take care of it and I won't have to think about it."

"What else is there to think about?"

"That question says it all," he said, delighted.

"But really, what else is there?"

"Oh, man things. You know. Our little dreams of glory."

He added a short laugh to show he knew such dreams hardly ever worked out: "Ha!"

He was all wound up on the subject, excited, like he was drawing her a map of the Promised Land. He must have given it a lot of thought. "And you put all the rest in *my* hands and you don't have to think about that."

"Like what?"

"Well, the divorces are an example. You left all that to me and I took care of everything."

"I was so glad you did that. I wouldn't've known where to begin."

"I know. Wherever the outside world touches us, that's up to me. You're the Angel of the Hearth, I'm the one who goes out and hunts the buffalo."

"That's beautiful! The Angel of the Hearth!" she said.

"I take care of the world around us. I got us this place. I take care of the car and the taxes. It's nothing you're not glad to leave to me. In the absence of buffalos, I bring in money and manage it. Money is in the public area."

Why did that scare her? Barney wasn't like Earl. Barney really did bring in money and really did share it. She didn't even have to ask for it. He deposited it in her checking account and gave her the deposit slip so she'd know. When he balanced her checkbook, he was never mad when he said she had paid too much for something or shouldn't have bought it just yet. There was always a warm little chuckle in his voice when he said things like that. She had never handled money, except in the restaurant. Of course he had to teach her.

He looked at his watch and jumped up. "I've got to stop running my mouth and hit the books," he said.

Trudi washed dishes, missing Ada, missing the restaurant. If she'd had a friend like Ada near by, she'd have started another. Close to the campus, maybe, where students would come. Students could be hired to mop up and take out the garbage. Wash dishes. People could phone in orders and students would deliver. Fine reliable students, older veterans, could be left in charge so she would have time at home to take care of Barney. He wouldn't be neglected at all. This restaurant, like the first one, would have a joint checking account.

Then she knew why she felt like she was on the roof and somebody was messing with her ladder.

There was Barney under his lamp, trying to write lists from memory. The room was so big he seemed to be in the middle of a field with one flickering candle. She shouldn't interrupt him, but she would.

Still carrying her dish towel, she said, "Why don't we have a joint account?"

"What?" He was miles away.

"A joint account."

"Why are you bringing this up now? We can talk about it later."

"Do you think I'd go on a spree and clean you out, is that what you think?"

"Have I been ungenerous? What is this? I thought you'd like having your own household account."

"But you just put what you want into it." She wasn't saying this right.

"What if I do? We just talked about that."

"It's like even if I went on a spree with it, it's just a certain amount that wouldn't matter. It's like you gave me a toy steering wheel and let me think I was driving."

"I really don't understand, honey," he said.

She was racking her brain for better words when the phone rang. How could it ring? It never rang. "The kids!" they both whispered at once and made a dash for it. Would they ever be able to hear it ring without thinking something bad had happened to their kids? She had a head start so she beat him by a step and gasped, "Hello?"

"Hey, Trudi," Ada said. "Guess whose husband got home from the wars and decided to go to Michigan State."

"Ada! Hi!" Trudi cried. She made an "it's okay" gesture to Barney but he stood right there.

Ada said, "We're all three living in the damnedest little shitbox you ever saw. It's sort of a housetrailer but it's got no wheels. We bring in water in a pail."

"We almost got one of those," Trudi said.

"Those what?" Barney said. Shouldn't he be making lists?

Ada said, "Then you know why I've got to make some money."

"I have to, too," Trudi said.

"You have to what too?" Barney said. She shook her head and smiled into the telephone.

Ada said, "So let's put on our chef hats and start over."

"Oh, let's! I've still got mine," Trudi said.

"Your what?" Barney said.

"My chef hat."

"Hey, wait a minute!" he said.

"Ada, can I call you back?"

But Ada was in a phone booth with a line of pregnant women waiting. She'd have to call again next day.

It should not have taken more than a minute to make Barney see what a godsend Ada was and be glad for Trudi's sake, if not entirely for his own. Yes, she'd be busy—but not too busy for him, never too busy for her darling. He would hardly notice, being busy too. And shouldn't he, right now, be studying? "How can I?" he said, hopelessly.

Why was his mind made up before he listened? Why wouldn't he listen? He brushed aside the mature, responsible veterans she and Ada would hire, like there were no such people, and sat there looking miserable and mulish, his ears laid back. He sat there for a long time like that, while Trudi paced back and forth, explaining. She suspected his head had gone white inside. She suspected him of a plan to hold his breath and die.

She stopped in front of him. "Listen," she said, "give us six months. In six months, if you can say you've been neglected, I'll quit. All right?"

Nobody could say that wasn't fair, except Barney. "Why should you care about me in six months, when you don't right now?" he said, all glum.

He refused to see that the restaurant had nothing to do with caring about him. She was *devoted* to him, couldn't he see? "You don't act like it," he said. "Why can't you trust me?"

"*Trust* you? But I do! You know I do! It's me I don't trust. I could get like I was before."

"You were perfect before. Ideal. Wonderful," he said. "I'd like to kill Owl for making you afraid to be like that. He should have honored you, as I do, and always did."

"I was a doormat. I was a beagle bitch. That's not what you like. You like women like Milly."

"Oh, my God! Is that it? You think I want you to be like Milly?"

How funny of him to say she didn't care for him, and turn right around and say she was doing what she did in hopes of pleasing him. "A little bit like Milly? Just some ways, not all?" she asked.

"No way. Not any way. I want you to be you—the real you—my Trude, that I always loved and wanted to help and wanted to rescue and take care of. Please be my Trude." He stood up and put his arms around her. "Please trust me to provide for you. Please trust me to be generous and fair."

"It's not that," she said, weakly.

"Yes it is. Please trust me not to be Owl."

"I know you're not him," she said, more weakly.

He had her cornered and he knew it. The more she didn't trust him, the more she had to pretend she did. Otherwise he wouldn't study and they wouldn't have a nice life or good times or anything. It was like he couldn't be a man if she didn't put everything she had into making him one. He must have felt the fight go out of her, felt her body go discouraged. He knew immediately that she had given in. "You won't be sorry," he said. "You're safe in my hands."

It might have ended like that, but he had to go and get a very satisfied expression—was *triumphant* the word?—just when she was feeling sorry for him because he'd stooped so low to get his own way. Far from being pitiful and embarrassed, he seemed to feel he had proved something wonderful about himself by getting the best of her, and even though she liked, in general, to make him happy, she never meant him to be happy *that* way, at her expense, *instead* of her. She liked surrendering to him, but she wanted it to be her own idea. He seemed to like it best when it was his idea and she didn't want to. She felt a little demon inside her stand up and look around. It felt like a tiny Pirate holding a dagger in its teeth.

The Pirate might have calmed down and disappeared— that look on Barney's face was just a flash, forgettable—but then Barney began to talk, and his words said the same things his face had. "There, there," he said, comfortingly, a big-hearted winner, sorry for her, "we win some, we lose some," and the Pirate brought out a tiny ladder and began climbing.

"We all make sacrifices for love," Barney said. "If you want to call taking care of me a sacrifice."

"What do you sacrifice?" she asked.

"You saw what I sacrificed for Milly."

The Pirate made a note about what a difference there was between what Barney had taken off Milly and what he would take off Trudi.

"I mean now," she said. "What about now?"

Funny, Barney couldn't feel the Pirate. Usually he knew

every change in her body, but he missed the Pirate, which was on her shoulder and about to stab him. Barney went galumphing on like a big happy dog in the snow. "Well, you know, most men are competing with each other, and women are just another weapon in that war, to impress other men. And I never did that, not with Milly and not with you. I went after what I really liked and really needed, personally."

"Some sacrifice," Trudi teased, smiling so he still didn't see the Pirate. "You don't do what you wouldn't want to anyway, and you get what you really want."

"Well, not all, of course. It depends on the priorities. You can have what you want most, but not what you want next most. And I want devotion. I want someone who'll take care of my private life, full time. Cheerfully. I've told you all that."

"What do you want next-most?"

He finally saw he was on thin ice and tried to back off. Too late. "Nothing of consequence," he said with a little aw-shucks chuckle. "Just to be handsome—strong—rich—wise. Little things like that," but she knew his sacrifice was *her*, a wife other men wouldn't envy him for.

Before the Pirate could leap at Barney's throat, she went to the bathroom to think. She might decide to let the Pirate do that, but she wanted to think about it first. If she wanted Barney to be fair, she had to be fair too. And was it fair to turn on him the first time he misspoke, after so many years of forgiving Earl no matter how many mean things he said and did on purpose? Poor Barney had just put his foot in it, accidentally—blurted out what they both knew was true, and so what? It wasn't like she'd ever thought of herself as a beauty queen or smart or whatever other men liked. Devotion, as a matter of fact, had always been her main pride. She could love. She could take care of the people she loved. So wasn't it nice of Barney to choose her for the very thing she loved herself best for, and not something imaginary that he might wake up from, even though Love is supposed to think you're better than you are?

So why was she so mad at him? Should she bury the mad, the way she was such an expert at, or should she go out and yell, the way the Pirate wanted, that Barney thought she was a natural-born slave but she wasn't and nobody is that's got something better to do? The Pirate said it would be exciting to yell, "If you want to mope your life away unless you have a slave, you can just go ahead and do it! It took me too long to crawl out. I'm not going back."

That Pirate had a big mouth. You don't have to say everything you think, or stab somebody you will probably feel better about soon. A middle way was needed, and Trudi sat thinking and thinking on the edge of the bathtub until a middle way came to her.

* * * * *

Ada drove over the next day instead of phoning. The mansion impressed her, all right—Trudi had seen her stop, amazed, to check the address—but she walked through the huge wonderful rooms without once gawking at anything. Back in the kitchen, she said, "Nice little place," patted back a ladylike yawn, and grinned. She liked to pretend to take good and bad the same. Do your best and worst, God: here stands Ada on her two solid feet.

"I've missed you *so much!*" Trudi said, putting water on to boil for tea.

"Yeah," Ada said. She spread out her want-ads, which were marked with several green-crayon circles under Business Opportunities. "We should get as close to the campus as we can. I missed you too. I don't know what got into me. Patriotism, I guess. Big war hero man, little piddly civilian woman me. Did I say what I wanted? No, I had to be noble.

I could have made it a little hard for you. It was awful when you left."

"It didn't work out with Persis?" Trudi asked, absolutely reeling with pleasure.

"She was okay. But she's got some prima donna in her. That's cute unless it's your partner. She wouldn't work nights. That got tiresome."

There went Trudi's middle way. Too bad she had let her pleasure show, because it left as fast as it came.

"*Now* what did I say?" Ada asked. It would be nice to have, just once, a feeling Ada didn't notice right away. "Have you been taking prima donna lessons? Do you think I shouldn't talk about people behind their back?"

"I just don't want this to be any bother to Barney," Trudi said.

"Uh oh," Ada said.

"Well, he wasn't too happy about it. I wasn't going to do it, in fact. Because he was so against it."

"Uh oh."

"Then I thought I could just work for you. I mean, you own it all and me not be a partner. And just do it when he's away. And not mention it. He's away all day, even Saturdays."

"You don't want to work nights?"

"Well, not at first. Until he sees it's no bother to him. Nights he just studies and I just rattle around. He'll see that."

"I haven't got money enough alone," Ada grumped.

"Oh, I could let you have some. But if I was a partner, I'd have to tell him. He'd have to sign something, wouldn't he?"

"Yeah," Ada sighed.

"Oh, Ada, let me! I haven't been myself."

Trudi could see Ada knowing all the unsaid things.

Ada was quiet a while, scarily long, but finally she said, "Why the hell not?" and they laughed and whirled each other around and Trudi told all her plans about mature responsible veterans and phone-in orders and home delivery. They left their teacups almost full and went out looking for a place. They didn't find one that day, but they would. The world felt big and interesting again.

Back home, getting out of Ada's car, Trudi turned and said, "Ada, you know how men always say women are sneaky? Am I being sneaky like they say?"

"Damn right, and about time, too. That's how men run their politics and wars and businesses. First they say they won't do it. Then they do it and say they're not. Then they say, well, they're doing it, but just a little. Then they say, well, they're doing it but there's too much invested to back out *now*. That's the only way anything gets done. They've been afraid we'd figure it out."

"Ada, you're the limit," Trudi said and laughed. When it was too late for Ada to back out, Trudi would tell her she also needed one weekend a month when the kids came.

Trudi smiled all through fixing Barney's supper, thinking about sneakiness and friendship and money and love, thinking maybe when Barney found out he'd be so mad he wouldn't make love anymore, but in that case maybe Ada would. The world's bigger and more interesting than you might think.

POSTSCRIPT: MILLY

It was hard to convince the children that Barney had a right to go back to school, to change jobs, to love Aunt Trude or anyone else he chose, to make a new start, to be happy. They said he had *them*, didn't he? Wasn't that happy enough? Surely, she told them, they didn't want to be his whole life. How about when they grew up? Did they want him to say, "*You* can't grow up and go away—you're my whole life?" That was too abstract for them so next Milly would whine, grasping their arms like an old man with trembling claws, "You can't play kickball, I want you to sit right here beside me," and that got through, sort of— enough to make them say "Yuck!" and decide to pretend Barney was still in the Navy.

Next day at dinner and sometimes again at bedtime, the whole exchange would start again with one of them saying, "I don't see why Daddy went away," indignantly, not many tears. Even Jack, certain Barney was his father too, was indignant. Sometimes they'd say if she hadn't got fat, Daddy would still love her and none of this would have happened. (She hoped that was what the general gossip was.) "He loves me and he loves all of you, but he has a right," she'd say. Over the course of weeks the yucks got more perfunctory and then days began to pass with nothing said. She began to breathe easier. No matter how much they might want to keep their grievances uppermost, they could not do it. Nature had aimed them forward. They were healthy animals built to go.

Barney was the easy part. Sooner or later they'd wonder what she and Lil were up to, and Milly intended to tell the truth if they were old enough by then to hear it. Having Barney's rights well in mind might make it possible for them to entertain the idea that Milly had some rights. It could go that way. It could be all right.

Meanwhile, they clung too much. They got up in the night to make sure she hadn't left too. She and Lil dared not sleep together. They lurked in wait for each other, pulled each other into shadows for quick kisses, quick touches to the nipples. There were secret grabs of the crotch when nobody was looking. Tracing the bottom's crack with a quick finger and looking away, all innocence. Uninvited comes, the cries stifled with a cautious forearm. Those times Milly thought she wouldn't have it any other way, but when, every month, they took the kids (Jack and Earl Junior too) for a weekend with Barney and Trude and drove back alone, they had to stop at a motel because all that foreplay was coming home to roost.

Barney and Trude were happy too. That is, they were

as happy as necessary. Earth is not heaven, as Milly had told Barney many times, back when she didn't know better.

He had got his heart's wish, a wife able to be a wife, and then when he'd been the focus of all the devotion an adult could endure, the gods relented, perhaps in recognition of his war service, and backed Trude away to breathing distance. How lucky can you get? He would come to be glad. He wasn't yet. Sometimes he phoned Milly, out of old simple habit. He'd open by bitching about Trude ("I shouldn't have to *think* about this stuff. Marriage is supposed to *settle* all that") but end up telling Milly, excited, what he was learning, which dear Trude couldn't make head or tail of and didn't want to.

"How do you diagnose Ada?" he asked sometimes. "Is she or isn't she?"

"How do I know?"

"Don't you people have an instinct?"

Milly's instinct about Ada was *yes*, but she didn't tell him that. Let him keep his damn fantasy out of it. He might be able to love Trude without it.

Trude had got her heart's wish too, a sexy husband and children grateful for a good breakfast, but she had looked timid for a while. There had been something of the old scurry in her walk, but she was scurry-free and sassy again, full of laughs and stories, though she was, as Lil said, busier than a one-armed butch and could often be found on Friday evenings soaking her feet. Something new had been added, possibly just money of her own. If it was Ada's love, Trude would tell Milly in her own good time. Sooner or later, you have to speak of the most beautiful thing in your life.

All in all, Milly felt guardedly hopeful. It appeared that happiness, though not mandated, was permitted. Love was possible and could be fairly durable. The children would probably forgive her, but even if they didn't—if they ran to Freud and tattled on her—hadn't she always wanted to be a star?

Best would be playing leathery old matriarch with Lil co-starring as co-matriarch. Children and grandchildren pouring into and pouring out of their house and their life, free to do either. Room, time, love enough for everybody. She'd better get busy on wisdom, in case the part required it.

THE END

Also of interest:

Isabel Miller
Patience and Sarah

'A beautifully written lesbian love story.' *Cosmopolitan*

Patience and Sarah met in Connecticut in 1816. Within days they were lovers...

Based on the lives of American painter Mary Ann Willson and her companion Miss Brundidge, who farmed, lived and loved together in the early nineteenth century, *Patience and Sarah* is a literary and lesbian classic. Published by Isabel Miller herself in 1969 when she was unable to find a publisher daring enough to take it on, this much-loved book is now an enduring international bestseller.

'Funny and true and tender, emotionally and physically erotic.' *Literary Review*

'This book is a real find.' *Good Housekeeping*

Fiction £5.99

Isabel Miller
A Dooryard Full of Flowers

From the writer of one of the most cherished books of all time comes the enchanting continuation of her classic story, *Patience and Sarah*. Now, in *A Dooryard Full of Flowers*, Isabel Miller offers long-awaited glimpses of their 'slow, ardent, exalted life together'.

And meet here too the married woman who falls in love with her mother-in-law, a woman in the navy determined that this time she will *not* fall for her new bunkmate, and a woman who finally comes face-to-face with her long-term penpal with unexpected results...

'There is a sense of authenticity which transcends fiction. Much the same can be said for her characters, who move through life with an almost stately grace. Most are seekers, women looking for love in all its guises...Their issues are the internal struggles of women, transcending time and era.' *Lambda Book Report*

Fiction £6.99

May Sarton
Mrs Stevens Hears the Mermaids Singing

Internationally acclaimed for her novels, *The Magnificent Spinster*, *The Education of Harriet Hatfield*, *A Reckoning* and *Kinds of Love*, as well as for her bestselling journals, this classic and much-loved novel has a special significance both to the author herself and to her readers. It is the first in which May Sarton wrote openly about homosexual love.

Hilary Stevens, a formidable personality and renowned poet, is in her seventies. But her hard-worn peace is disrupted first by an angry young poet, Mar, and then by two journalists seeking the source of her inspiration. In the course of her interview with them, and as her relationship with Mar develops, Hilary Stevens finally comes to terms with her own past and her creative muse.

'May Sarton ranks with the very best of distinguished novelists. The reader is compelled to that feeling of awe which the accomplishments of first-rate literary creation inevitably bring forth.' *New York Times Book Review*

Fiction £5.99